Click: An Online Love Story

Lisa Becker

This is a work of fiction. All names, places and incidents, other than those which are in the public domain, are the product of the author's imagination or are used fictitiously and any resemblance to actual persons, living or dead, businesses, events or locales is entirely coincidental.

For SJB, my soul mate, and OJB and MJB, the loves of my life

With gratitude to JR and GSD, for without you,
life as I know it would not exist

With gratitude to mom and dad, for without you, *I* would not exist

Special thanks to TMZ and LA for their professional expertise

CHAPTER ONE – PRETTY PLEASE!!!!

From: Mark Finlay – January 2, 2011 – 9:03 AM
To: Renee Greene
Subject: Pretty Please!!!!

Thanks for staying late to help me clean up yesterday. You know I just can't go to sleep with dirty dishes in the sink, streamers on the walls, empty champagne bottles that need recycling, dirt tracked onto the hard wood floors, etc. You know me. ;) You're a real pal. Oh, Ralph really liked Shelley. He plans to give her a call this week. He really thinks she could be "the one," but don't tell her I told you.

Okay. Now to the subject of this email. I know you will think I'm a major loser and a dork – not that you already don't ;) – but my New Year's resolution is to try an online dating service and I don't want to do it alone. I know this year will be a busy one for me, trying to develop the cell phone game sequel, but I also feel like it's the right time to meet the right girl. Hence, Pretty Please!!!! Come on – it will be a great way to meet new people and you never know, the man of your dreams may be hooked up to a UNIX system right now. Pretty Please!!!!

From: Renee Greene – January 3, 2011 – 9:16 AM
To: Shelley Manning
Subject: Fwd: Pretty Please!!!!

Have I really gotten this desperate? I know I promised myself that I would try anything if I wasn't married, engaged, seriously dating, had a prospect or at least a house full of cats, by my 30th birthday. Well, with 25 days to go, do I dive in this way? Help?

Oh, by the way. Ralph seems to think you are "the one."
One night stand is more like it…Tee Hee! ;)

From: Shelley Manning – January 3, 2011 – 9:38 AM
To: Renee Greene
Subject: Re: Fwd: Pretty Please!!!!

Poor Ralphie. Poor stupid Ralphie. Well despite the raging hangover and Finlay's anal retentive tendencies, it was a great party. But, it's a party for Christ's sake. Every time I put my drink down on the table, he was either throwing the cup in the trash or shooting me dirty looks for not using a coaster. That boy has got to light-en up! Talk about panties in a wad. What he needs is a good screw. Which leads me to your question. (Nice segue, huh?) As far as the online dating thing goes…**Yes, you are that desperate**. ;) I say give it a try. No harm. No foul. Finlay's right. (Don't tell him those words uttered from my lips – or in this case from my fingertips! He would never let me live it down!) You never know what might happen. At the very least, you'll have eligible men taking you to swank restaurants. Hmmm. A whole host of hot and horny single men that I can review, chat with, judge and mock – all while sitting in my office looking very busy. Maybe I should give it a try myself. Lunch tomorrow?

From: Renee Greene – January 3, 2011 – 9:43 AM
To: Shelley Manning
Subject: Re: Fwd: Pretty Please!!!!

Thank you for your generous contribution to the "Flatter Renee Greene's Ego Foundation." Next time, don't be such a tight wad. Okay, I'll give it a whirl. But you have to promise – I mean <u>promise</u> on a box of cupcakes and a jar of anti-wrinkle cream – that you won't tell anyone. Not a soul.

Lunch tomorrow is great. Meet you at Mel's at 12:30.

From: Shelley Manning – January 3, 2011 – 9:58 AM
To: Renee Greene
Subject: Re: Fwd: Pretty Please!!!!

Of course I agree to keep the secret. If I couldn't keep a secret, then everyone would already know about that time you danced topless on a Cancun tabletop during spring break. I even have the pictures to prove it. Oh yes, there are photos. Multiple photos. They are tucked safely away in a Swiss safe deposit vault. Only two people known to man have the keys. So, you are forever at my mercy. Mwah ha ha ha ha! (Picture me looking really evil with a maniacal tone in my voice as I say that. Much better in person. Trust me.) Now of course if my emails from work are being monitored, I can't accept responsibility for spilling the beans. But, I think the evil corporate trolls here have better things to do than worry about your dating life. Right? Okay. Gotta go. There is a really hot new senior manager that just transferred here from the New York office. Too bad he's not in the HR department. I wouldn't mind being assigned under him…or over him. Whatever his pleasure. ;) Good thing I work in HR and understand the importance of not making harassing, disparaging or inappropriate comments in the workplace. :) Regardless, I've got to go through some paperwork with him. Mwah! Mwah!

From: Renee Greene – January 3, 2011 – 11:59 AM
To: Mark Finlay
Subject: Re: Pretty Please!!!!

Sorry so late in responding. Didn't check my work email over the weekend. My response: Ugh! I'm not certain I want to be with a man that even knows what a UNIX system is. But, I guess UNIX is better than Eunuchs. Ha! Ha! Okay, obviously this situation is making me a bit uncomfortable and as a result I've resorted to homonym humor. But I do crack myself up. Okay. I apologize. Please disregard. Okay, I'm in. Feeling a bit desperate, but willing to give it a shot. What do I need to do?

From: Shelley Manning – January 3, 2011 – 2:02 PM
To: Renee Greene
Subject: Re: Fwd: Pretty Please!!!!

Okay, so the new guy isn't as hot as I thought. I guess when you get a three-second glimpse of someone walking down the hall through a small glass partition in a conference room, it's hard to make a solid judgment. But, he's pretty cute, in a preppy kind of way. He's got really nice blue eyes, too. From now on, he will be here to forth known as Preppy Dude. We're going for drinks after work tonight. So, did Finlay pee himself when you said you would do this online dating thing with him?

From: Ashley Price – January 3, 2011 – 4:45 PM
To: Renee Greene
Subject: Convent Bound

Sister Mary Catherine, my old teacher at St. Francis' Sunday school, had the right idea. I'm convinced I was destined to be a nun, because there is NO ONE GOOD LEFT. I just don't know what to do anymore. New Year's was a disaster. Evan and I are over…for good this time.

It started out fine enough. He came by to pick me up and was 20 minutes late. Okay, I thought. I could let this slide…again. But really, is it too much to ask my boyfriend to show up on time, especially when we were going to "the club?" So, I asked him why it was so hard to pick me up on time and it just spiraled from there.

Oh, did I mention that his tuxedo pants were too short? I told him he should buy, not rent, but he just doesn't listen.

So anyway, we're arguing in the car and I ask that he please just make an effort. It's New Years, the annual ball, and he's meeting all of my parents' friends for the first time for goodness sake. And I know I'm a little stressed out. I mean, I really want everyone to like him. And what's not to like, right? He's smart and comes from a good family. I mean granted, he could do a lot more than be a teacher. I know he likes teaching in the inner city and gets a lot of satisfaction from it, but he could be a lawyer or a doctor. But he's pursuing his heart, right?

Well, he proceeds to hit on the waitress (a waitress!?!), get WILDLY drunk and PASS OUT in the men's room. I've never been more mortified. But you would have been proud. It was like a scene from a movie. I poured a champagne bucket of ice water over his head and told him we were through. My parents drove me home.

I'm okay now. I realize we just weren't right for each other. And I know I deserve better. So, I'm giving up on dating. That's it. I'm resigning myself to a life of loneliness and solitude.

How was Mark's party? Did you have fun?

From: Renee Greene – January 3, 2011 – 5:00 PM
To: Ashley Price
Subject: Re: Convent Bound

I'm so sorry, Ashley. I know you were really hoping it would work out this time. Don't give up. There's someone out there just perfect for you. We all had a good time at Mark's party. Shelley and I are meeting tomorrow for lunch…12:30 at Mel's. Why don't you meet us there?

From: Ashley Price – January 3, 2011 – 5:15 PM
To: Renee Greene
Subject: Re: Convent Bound

I have a lunch meeting tomorrow. Besides, no offense, but I just don't think I could stand to hear more of Shelley's sex-capades. Especially not now. Just reminds me that men come (yes, pun absolutely intended) and then they go. Sorry I'm so depressing. I'll call you later.

From: Mark Finlay – January 4, 2011 – 2:33 PM
To: Renee Greene
Subject: Site Selection

Great! Glad you will embark on this journey with me. So, I've investigated the top 20 online dating sites on the Internet and culled the list down to the best four for you.

Now you'll need to choose from there based on this list of pros and cons I prepared.

Dating World

PROS: They have thousands of members locally or globally in case you want to meet someone in Katmandu. It's the fastest growing dating site. I even looked them up in Consumer Reports and they were rated #1. It's also completely free, which is great but has a downside. All of the cheapies come here.
CONS: Well, besides the aforementioned, you have to wade through ads, which makes the service free.

Choose Jews

PROS: All of the men are Jewish. Your mother will be thrilled. All of those nice Jewish boys. She always told me if I only were Jewish, than you and I could be together. Oy! Only $20 a month and you get lots of anonymity.
CONS: All of the men are Jewish. HA! Just kidding. I know how you feel about the pressure to marry a Jew, keep the religion alive, etc.

SciBer Love

PROS: Does scientific matches. (Hence the SciBer instead of Cyber. Kind of clever, but a bit intellectual. Not sure the masses will really get it.) So you have a better chance of meeting someone who is a good fit.
CONS: No photos allowed. I think online dating should have similar security to the airlines these days, where a current photo ID is required.

Mode

PROS: Geared toward the hip, affluent crowd. This is the site for the beautiful people.

CONS: This is the site for the beautiful people. Not that we aren't beautiful, but do we really want to limit the dating pool to pretentious, wannabe actors/actresses in LA? $60 a month. Guess they want to weed out the undesirables, or at least the ones with small balance sheets.

I can send you my thoughts on the other sites if none of these seem to meet your needs. I'm still trying to figure out which one makes the most sense for me.

Once you pick a site, you'll need to write a profile. Profile formats vary by site. You'll probably need to put in some personal basics, choose from a list of interests and then write some brief essays. Let me know if you have any questions.

From: Renee Greene – January 4, 2011 – 4:59 PM
To: Shelley Manning
Subject: Re: Fwd: Pretty Please!!!!

Mark was quite pleased and in true "Finlay Fashion" - as you would call it - has already reviewed all of the top sites and provided me with a pros and cons list of each that would be best for me. What have I gotten myself into? Not the online dating thing. No, I'm talking about entering a project with Mark.

You know I love him. Have ever since the 7th grade when he alphabetized my bat mitzvah invitations for me and set up a spreadsheet for me to track thank you notes. But the boy is so ANAL. Have fun with Preppy Dude. Don't do anything I wouldn't do. Oh wait. Considering I haven't been on a date in over a year, that would rule out much of anything fun. And Lord knows, you like to have fun ;)

From: Shelley Manning – January 4, 2011 – 5:03 PM
To: Renee Greene
Subject: Re: Fwd: Pretty Please!!!!

Damn right I do!

From: Renee Greene – January 5, 2011 – 8:58 AM
To: Shelley Manning
Subject: The Scoop

So, what happened with Preppy Dude last night? Good time? Do tell. You know I live vicariously through you. Details!!!

From: Shelley Manning – January 5, 2011 – 9:25 AM
To: Renee Greene
Subject: Re: The Scoop

Mixed reviews. The good news. Great sex!!! Who knew he had it in him. Or should I say in me. HA! (I think I've been watching too many "Sex in the City" reruns.) Anyway, the bad news: He's a - I shudder the thought - CUDDLER. You know how I HATE that. Why, oh why must such an amazing romp be spoiled by the heinous act of cuddling. UGH! But, I think I can break him of the habit. At least I'm going to try. It would be well worth it. Trust me. Mwah! Mwah!

From: Renee Greene – January 5, 2011 – 9:43 AM
To: Shelley Manning
Subject: Re: The Scoop

How horrible for you. A cuddler. <Insert sarcastic tone>. Great sex and someone who doesn't want to jump out of bed and go home. <Yes, more sarcasm.>

Sorry. I just don't know how you are constantly meeting these men when I've resorted to whittling down my life to a few short paragraphs so as to intrigue a man to want to talk with me further. Sorry. Turning 30 and no one to take me out is a bit depressing.

From: Shelley Manning – January 5, 2011 – 9:48 AM
To: Renee Greene
Subject: Re: The Scoop

What do you mean, no one to take you out? Okay, I'll admit that Finlay IS chopped liver. Well, a goyish version of chopped liver. But, I'm certainly caviar with a mojito on the side.

From: Renee Greene – January 5, 2011 – 9:54 AM
To: Shelley Manning
Subject: Re: The Scoop

I know. You guys are great. Ashley's coming too, along with a group of friends from work. I don't mean to sound ungrateful. I guess when I look back, I always thought that by 30 I'd be married with three kids. And here I am, with a few weeks to go, and I'm not even dating anyone. Okay, pity party of one, here. Sorry.

From: Shelley Manning – January 5, 2011 – 9:59 AM
To: Renee Greene
Subject: Re: The Scoop

So, Ashley's coming. Great. Miss Priss. That'll make for a fun evening.

But on to important matters. You are a truly wonderful woman and person. You will meet someone. You will get married. You will have your three kids. You just need to have faith and you just need to get out there. You're never going to meet someone sitting at home and lamenting over Derrick. It's been over a year and you haven't gotten on with things. I don't mean to sound harsh (unless we're talking about Miss Priss of course) but it's time for some tough love - not the S&M kind although that could be fun ;) - and I do love you.

From: Renee Greene – January 5, 2011 – 10:05 AM
To: Shelley Manning
Subject: Re: The Scoop

It's PRICE not Priss. You are the devil incarnate. No, I know. You're right. It's just easier to sit at home, eat cupcakes and feel sorry for myself than risk getting hurt. But, it's a new year and a new plan.

From: Shelley Manning – January 5, 2011 – 10:07 AM
To: Renee Greene
Subject: Re: The Scoop

Priss, Price. Same difference. :) See you at 12:30.

From: Renee Greene – January 5, 2011 – 1:58 PM
To: Shelley Manning
Subject: How do you do it?!?

I just don't get it. I mean don't get me wrong. You're awesome. But, I just don't know how you do it. That handsome, wannabe actor, underwear-model-looking waiter was just gushing over you.

And don't think I didn't see him slip you his number. Good looking, yes. Subtle and bright, no. Greene may be my last name, but it is an ugly color on me. UGH!

So, are you going to call him, or are you getting serious with the Cuddler? HA! I just laughed out loud as I was typing that. No offense or anything. First of all, don't see you getting serious with ANYONE, let alone some lame, girly guy.

From: Shelley Manning – January 5, 2011 – 2:43 PM
To: Renee Greene
Subject: Re: How do you do it?!?

No offense taken. You're right. I'm not interested in getting serious with anyone. Why settle down when I'm having so much fun? So, handsome, wannabe actor, underwear-model-looking waiter, here I come. And, hopefully, when I say here I come…well you're a smart girl, you know where this is heading. (HA! An unintentional pun, to boot.)

And, speaking of being a smart girl, how many times do I need to tell you how beautiful, witty, charming and fabulous you are? You are Supermodel Renee, for Christ's sake! You just need to start believing it yourself. No more of this pity shit. Get over it. Okay!!!!???

From: Renee Greene – January 5, 2011 – 3:30 PM
To: Shelley Manning
Subject: Re: How do you do it?!?

Yes ma'am! Will do my best.

From: Ashley Price – January 6, 2011 – 9:07 AM
To: Renee Greene
Subject: Lunch scoop

So, how was lunch at Mel's? How many guys did Shelley pick up? How much sex is she having?

On another note, Evan called, apologized, sent flowers, etc. etc. But this time I'm not falling for it. It's over.

From: Renee Greene – January 6, 2011 – 3:12 PM
To: Ashley Price
Subject: Re: Lunch scoop

Lunch was typical as usual. There is a new waiter there who was incredibly hot and incredibly into Shelley. New year, but nothing's new. You know I love her, but it's hard being the girl guys always approach in bars only to say, "Hi. Who's your friend?"

Yes, you deserve far better than Evan. What you need to do is erase his phone number from your cell, don't answer his calls and texts, send back the flowers, etc. I mean he's a decent guy and all, but you just never seem happy when you're with him. At the end of the day, I just want you to be happy.

From: Ashley Price – January 6, 2011 – 4:45 PM
To: Renee Greene
Subject: Re: Lunch scoop

I know. I know. I'm NOT going to call him back.

Regarding Shelley, yes, I know you are very loyal to her and she's certainly been a good friend. But if I were a guy, I would pick you over her in a heartbeat. You've got style, class and a great sense of humor. Just need to try something new with your hair. So, buck up. This is a new year and I feel like good things are just around the corner for you. Gotta run. Work beckons.

From: Renee Greene – January 9, 2011 – 3:36 PM
To: Mark Finlay
Subject: Re: Site Selection

Okay, Mark. I don't think I could live with the Jewish guilt by bringing home someone who couldn't appreciate a good corned beef sandwich or my bubbies matzo ball soup. So, Choose Jews it is. I'm going to write my profile this weekend and will be emailing it to them. Thanks for pushing me into doing this. I think it's going to be good for me.

From: Mark Finlay – January 9, 2011 – 5:55 PM
To: Renee Greene
Subject: Re: Site Selection

I always know what's good for you. Why you haven't figured that out by now is beyond me. Well, I've narrowed down my list of prospective services down to four. Still doing a bit of research and getting a few references for each. With my future wife on the line, you just can't be too careful.

From: Renee Greene – January 13, 2011 – 11:35 PM
To: member.services@choosejews.com
Bcc: Shelley Manning, Mark Finlay
Subject: Profile for Site

I'm a new member…Renee Greene. Here is my completed profile. My ID# is 49628; Screen Name: PRGal1981. Thanks!

AGE: 29
HEIGHT: 5'1"
EYES: Brown
HAIR: Brown
ASTROLOGICAL SIGN: Taurus
AFFILIATION: Reform

FAVORITE CUISINE: Italian, Caribbean, California-Fusion, Chinese/Dim Sum, Japanese/Sushi, Middle Eastern Barbecue, Deli, French, Greek, Indian, Mexican, Middle Eastern, Thai, Cajun/Southern, Continental, Eastern European, Mediterranean

INTERESTS: art galleries, theatre, restaurants, movies, comedy clubs, museums, concerts, bookstores, shopping malls, intimate conversations, cooking, listening to music, shopping, traveling, watching videos, hanging out with friends, taking long walks, wine tasting, antique stores/flea markets, reading, coffee houses

MY PERSONALITY TRAITS: friendly, kind, artistic, easygoing, flexible, humorous, intellectual, nurturing, romantic, sensitive, talkative, witty

OCCUPATION: Public Relations Director

MORE ABOUT ME: I've never been *really* comfortable talking about myself. So, in an effort to seem incredibly modest, I thought it would be better to share what I think *other* people would say about me. My parents would describe me as loving, compassionate and fiercely independent. My friends would say I'm fun, easy going, funny and incredibly loyal. My co-workers and boss would say I'm smart, savvy and ambitious in my career. My nephew would say I'm incredibly silly, but play a highly-competitive game of "Chutes and Ladders." Other things about me of interest: I cry at Hallmark commercials, love the band Spider Fire, enjoy baking and cooking (and make the world's greatest chocolate chip cookies – no exaggeration here!), sing (sometimes off key) with the radio while driving, own more pairs of black shoes than should be legal, and my fear of flying is rivalled only by my love for chocolate.

WHAT I'VE LEARNED FROM PAST RELATIONSHIPS: Maybe the toilet seat should be up. SportsCenter on ESPN is funny. No, these pants do NOT make me look fat. Which one is Beavis and which is Butthead. Asking for directions IS bad. Seriously, I've learned that you need to be honest, forgiving and willing to communicate for a relationship to succeed. And a sense of humor and ability to laugh at yourself goes a long way.

CHAPTER TWO – UNSUITABLE SUITORS

From: member.services@choosejews.com – January 14, 2011 – 1:03 AM
To: Renee Greene
Bcc: Shelley Manning, Mark Finlay
Subject: Re: Profile for Site

Thank you for submitting your profile to Choose Jews, the number one dating website for the Jewish community. Your screen name is <PRGal1981>. As other members become interested in communicating with you, they will email you at meet@choosejews.com/PRGal1981. To read the message, simply login to the site using your ID number and confidential password <*****>. Click on the message to open. You will see the member's profile and photo below their initial message. If you decide to write back, simply click "reply" in the member's note, write your own note and send. All communications with other members stay on the Choose Jews Web site so that you never have to give out any personal information. When you are comfortable, you can exchange personal information with other members. Thank you for selecting our service. Please contact member.services@choosejews.com with any questions.

From: meet@choosejews.com/L'Chiam22 – January 14, 2011 – 5:54 AM
To: meet@choosejews.com/PRGal1981
Subject: Shalom

Shalom, PRGal1981. Don't know your real name…yet :)

You seem like a really smart and interesting person and I think we would have a lot in common. I'm originally from New York – Queens to be specific – but made Alliyah to Israel a little more than 8 years ago. I had visited when I was 13 for my Bar Mitzvah and felt a spiritual connection to the land and to my people. So, when an opportunity came up to transfer from the Internet company I worked for to the Tel Aviv office, I jumped at it. When the Internet boom went bust, so did my job. But I decided to stay and found work as a computer engineer for a software developer.

I live in Tel Aviv and am looking for a spiritual woman to share a Jewish life with.

From: Renee Greene – January 14, 2011 – 9:04 AM
To: Shelley Manning
Subject: Fwd: Shalom

Okay, so I sent my profile in last night and thought I would take a chance that someone emailed me this morning. Yes, I know that seems egotistical thinking that someone would email me so quickly after my profile was posted. And considering it didn't officially go online until 1:00 am, I'm not sure I want to date anyone who was trolling the Internet for a date in the wee hours of the morning. But, to be honest, I'm kind of excited about the possibilities. Imagine that. Me…being hopeful. Who knew? Anyway, I was elated – yes, elated – to find I had a message. Hurrah! Then I read it. He is very religious, is looking for a "spiritual" woman and lives in Israel. Good lord! (HA! Maybe that does indeed make me "spiritual" enough for this guy.) Israel!!!

Okay, don't get me wrong. I have nothing against Israel. I am one of the Chosen People after all. And, apparently "chosen" in more ways than one, huh? But do you picture me living in an area where 1) Most people take the bus – I'm from LA for goodness sake, where we LIVE in our cars. In fact, I have this theory that no one walks in LA. But, we all own treadmills. So, even though it is nice all year long, we won't walk outside. We'd rather walk in our houses. But, I digress. Back to what's important here: 2) These buses blow up into fiery messes; 3) And speaking of fiery messes, it is hot in Israel. Yes, yes. It's a dry heat. But you know what? A blast furnace is a dry heat. But it's still HOT and I wouldn't want to live in it. Yeah, right. Like I'm going to start a relationship with some man in Israel.

And, he is so intense about Judaism. I haven't been to temple since my nephew's baby naming three years ago. Oh, this would NEVER work. NEVER.

So, how do I get out of this? Do I ignore his message? Do I email back and say thanks but no thanks? Yikes! I'm not sure what to do?

From: Shelley Manning – January 14, 2011 – 10:45 AM
To: Renee Greene
Subject: Re: Fwd: Shalom

Step 1. Revise your profile. No spiritual junkies or out of towners accepted.
Step 2. Email him back and tell him you are not interested in a long distance thing.
Step 3. Laugh your ass off. He obviously does NOT know you.

Okay. So this one isn't going to work out. But, to your point, it's only been a few hours. And, in this man's defense, it's probably not 1:00 am his time. It's like two days later and early evening or something. So, it is flattering that he thinks you are the funny, smart and…okay, maybe not "spiritual" but certainly awesome…person that you really are. You're going to get a TON of emails and have your pick of tons of great guys. Just you wait. Trust me.

Speaking of great guy, going out again with The Cuddler tonight. Hoping to break him of his bad habits. I'm willing to use force if necessary. Hope he likes it rough ;) Gotta run. Evil corporate trolls demanding reports. Call me tonight. Mwah! Mwah!

From: meet@choosejews.com/PRGal1981 – January 14, 2011 – 11:30 AM
To: meet@choosejews.com/ L'Chiam22
Bcc: Shelley Manning
Subject: Shalom back

Dear L'Chiam22. Thank you very much for your nice email. I must confess yours is the first email I've received. It's quite flattering, especially to have someone from so far away take an interest. Thank you. But, I also must confess that I'm looking to meet someone local. So, best of luck in meeting that woman of your dreams. I'm sure she's out there.

From: Shelley Manning – January 14, 2011 – 11:34 AM
To: Renee Greene
Subject: Re: Shalom back

Nicely done, sweetie. Ever the diplomat.

From: Renee Greene – January 14, 2011 – 11:47 AM
To: Shelley Manning
Subject: Re: Shalom back

It's so much easier to reject someone over the Internet than in real life. Score one for online dating!

From: Renee Greene – January 14, 2011 – 1:36 PM
To: Mark Finlay
Subject: THE SCOOP!

Got my first email today from a gentleman suitor. It was a bit of a rush, I must say. But, he lives in Israel and I'm not really looking for a long distance thing. I don't even think I could date anyone who lived in the Valley. What about you? Lots of women clamoring over you? Do tell.

From: Mark Finlay – January 15, 2011 – 10:30 AM
To: Renee Greene
Subject: Re: THE SCOOP!

Oh, I'm still looking into services. I've narrowed it down to two based on referrals from people who have tried them. Also, I read on the Web that in a few weeks the new Consumer Reports comes out and rates the best online dating services. So, I'm going to wait and review the article before making a decision.

But, very excited for you. Go girl! Okay that sounds totally ridiculous coming from me, doesn't it? I'm just not one of those types who can get away with the slang expressions. So, let me rephrase. Good for you! I'm confident you are going to get a lot of emails. You're smart, pretty and lots of fun. Keep me posted.

Also, how many of us will there be for your birthday dinner. Also, do you have any place in mind, or do you want to be surprised? Either way, I want to be sure and get a reservation in.

From: Renee Greene – January 15, 2011 – 4:45 PM
To: Mark Finlay
Subject: Re: THE SCOOP!

Oh, surprise me. But, be warned. If I see one – and I mean one – "Over the Hill" decoration, gag gift or piece of paraphernalia, you will pay a very high price. A very high price indeed. You don't want me as an enemy. And you know I hold a grudge. Okay, so I'm not the best intimidator. Hard to be fierce and menacing when you stand 5'1" and look 12. But, I have to tell you, I'm finding this birthday a bit daunting. Turning 30 is always hailed as this depressing milestone. As someone going through it, to someone who has another six months to go, it's all true. This sucks!

From: Mark Finlay – January 16, 2011 – 12:10 PM
To: Renee Greene
Subject: Re: THE SCOOP!

I've been duly warned. And yes, I do know how you hold a grudge. When you've been friends with someone for more than 20 years, you learn all that kind of stuff.

From: Renee Greene – January 16, 2011 – 2:30 PM
To: Mark Finlay
Subject: Re: THE SCOOP!

Thanks. If I'm going to suffer the indignity of ungracefully entering old age, I'm glad I'll have my best buds there to watch me go kicking and screaming into my thirties. Okay, I'm being a bit (read: overwhelmingly) dramatic. It's in my nature. And, since you've known me for more than 20 years, you already know that. Okay, gotta run.

From: Mark Finlay – January 17, 2011 – 9:04 AM
To: Shelley Manning, Ashley Price, Renee Greene
Subject: Renee is turning six (and two dozen)

Yes, you read correctly. We are celebrating Renee's 6th (and two dozen) birthday. (I know you are displeased with entering your 30's, so I figured, why do it? Turn six…again.) So, to celebrate her 6th birthday, we are having the party at Pizza Party Zone near Culver City. Won't that be a ton of fun?!? We'll eat pizza, play arcade games and have our photo taken with the silly frog mascot. Check out this link to the evite. Hoping you can proofread it before I invite everyone?

From: Shelley Manning – January 17, 2011 – 9:10 AM
To: Renee Greene
Subject: Fwd: Renee is turning six (and two dozen)

Don't worry. I am now in charge of your birthday celebration. I will let Finlay know that we are NOT going to Pizza Party Zone. Just what you need…and we need. Screaming brats. Greasy pizza. Video games. What the HELL was Finlay thinking?

From: Renee Greene – January 17, 2011 – 9:15 AM
To: Shelley Manning
Subject: Re: Fwd: Renee is turning six (and two dozen)

Thank you. I just read Mark's email and started to have a bit of a panic attack. You're so lucky your birthday isn't until December. But, I'm surprised you don't want to go the Pizza Party Zone. With screaming brats come cute single dads. (Tee Hee!)

From: Shelley Manning – January 17, 2011 – 9:18 AM
To: Renee Greene
Subject: Re: Fwd: Renee is turning six (and two dozen)

Cute single dads? Pizza Party Zone, here we come. JUST KIDDING. Don't worry. I'll come up with something fab and perfectly fitting for this momentous occasion.

From: Shelley Manning – January 17, 2011 – 3:00 PM
To: Mark Finlay
Subject: Re: Renee is turning six (and two dozen)

Finlay! Renee does not want to go to Pizza Party Zone for her birthday. I'm sure she appreciated the sentiment, but I think she would prefer a quiet dinner with her closest friends. I've got us a reservation at Alex's on Melrose for 9:00. We can all meet at my place at 8:00 for a pre-dinner mojito. I'll let everyone know the plan.

From: meet@choosejews.com/OutdoorDude – January 17, 2011 – 4:03 PM
To: meet@choosejews.com/PRGal1981
Subject: Hello there

Hi there PRGal. My name is Kevin. I was checking out the site this morning and came across your profile. You seem like a really smart and outgoing person. As for me, I'm originally from Nebraska and have been living in LA for two years. I moved out here to try my luck at movies and ended up doing personal training for celebrities. But I got a bit fed up with the egos. So now I work as a counselor for Outward Adventure programs, which take at-risk youth, corporate teams and others on outdoor adventures. It's great to enjoy the sunshine and see how the challenges of nature and teamwork can change someone's life. When I'm not working, I'm usually working out, playing sports or taking a bike ride. I'm looking for someone who is going to be the perfect compliment to me. Check out my profile and see what you think. Will look forward to hearing back from you.

From: Renee Greene – January 18, 2011 – 9:25 AM
To: Shelley Manning; Mark Finlay
Subject: Fwd: Hello there

Well, things seem to be improving a bit. Got this email. He seems VERY ACTIVE, which is so not me. I don't see him sitting around watching a "Law & Order" marathon with me while I eat frosting from a can, which as you know is my idea of a good night. And, he has a grammatical error. I'm sure he meant to say he's looking for a "complement" to himself, not for someone to "compliment" him. That sounds more like Derrick. Yes, still bitter after a year, but what can I say? I do hold a grudge. Hey, but at least this Kevin guy is local. I'm getting closer. I'll let him down gently.

From: Shelley Manning – January 18, 2011 – 11:44 AM
To: Renee Greene
Subject: Re: Fwd: Hello there

He's hot. I bet he looks awesome without a shirt on. You should go out with him. Just because you guys are different doesn't mean you can't have fun. And, did I mention that he's hot? Okay, so forgot to tell you, the Cuddler and I are no more. He's a sweet guy but I've already had my fun and now it's time to move on. He hinted the same thing. Plus, I think he's been burned by a work affair before and seems gun shy about getting hurt again.

From: Renee Greene – January 18, 2011 – 11:59 AM
To: Shelley Manning
Subject: Re: Fwd: Hello there

Poor Cuddler. When you give his sensitive booty the boot, I bet he'll cry. HA! HA! I bet he will run home crying to his mommy. He probably shops at WimpsRUs. I could go on, but onto more important matters.

Well, Kevin may indeed be hot, and I could be tempted to take a peek at the pecs, but no. I know it would not work out, so I'm going to let him know that we just don't seem to have a lot in common. I can't go out with someone when I know there isn't a possibility for a future.

From: Shelley Manning – January 18, 2011 – 12:07 PM
To: Renee Greene
Subject: Re: Fwd: Hello there

Hilarious! But seriously sweetie. The Cuddler is not THAT bad. He was actually a great guy who just happened to enjoy the lingering cuddle and occasional spoon.

But, I love the jokes. Keep 'em coming. And, speaking of keeping 'em coming, I have a hot date tonight. Gotta get some work done for the evil corporate trolls. Mwah! Mwah!

From: Mark Finlay – January 18, 2011 – 3:00 PM
To: Shelley Manning; Renee Greene
Subject: Re: Fwd: Hello there

Let 'em down gently there, tiger.

From: meet@choosejews.com/PRGal1981 – January 18, 2011 – 4:02 PM
To: meet@choosejews.com/OutdoorDude
Bcc: Shelley Manning
Subject: Re: Hello there

Thanks so much for your email, Kevin. I did look through your profile. You seem like a really nice guy. And you also seem like you're looking for someone to share your love of the outdoors, interest in sports and thrill for adventure. I just don't think we're a right fit for each other. I'm really not the outdoorsy/active type. Good luck meeting someone else, though. I'm sure the perfect gal is out there waiting for you.

From: Mark Finlay – January 18, 2011 – 5:12 PM
To: Shelley Manning
Subject: Re: Renee is turning six (and two dozen)

No problem. Just trying to help her get over this ridiculous fear of turning 30. I just logged on and read three separate reviews of Alex's and it sounds great. See you then.

From: Shelley Manning – January 18, 2011 – 6:30 PM
Bcc: <undisclosed recipients>
Subject: Renee's Birthday

Here's the plan for Renee's birthday celebration. Meet at my place (Melrose near Highland, Apt. B) at 8:00 on Friday the 28th for a pre-dinner cocktail. We have a reservation at Alex's for 9:00. Come dressed WEST HOLLYWOOD CHIC. Let's be ready to celebrate our dear friend Renee's birthday in style.

From: Renee Greene – January 18, 2011 – 6:32 PM
To: Shelley Manning
Subject: Re: Renee's Birthday

THANK YOU! THANK YOU! I can't believe you got us a table at Alex's. I thought that place had a waiting list for months. You are wonderful and I'm very excited to celebrate with you guys. And thank you for being subtle about the dress code. I know you were really holding back.

From: meet@choosejews.com/OutdoorDude – January 20, 2011 – 2:45 PM
To: meet@choosejews.com/PRGal1981
Subject: Reconsider?

I don't understand why you don't think we would get along. I don't think you should be so quick to judge without getting to know me.

From: Renee Greene – January 20, 2011 – 2:54 PM
To: Shelley Manning
Subject: Fwd: Reconsider?

Okay, Shelley. I tried to be nice when I got his email and politely explained that we aren't a right fit. I mean everything in his profile screamed of sports and outdoors. That is just so not me. And, this is the response I get. I don't know what to say back. Help?

From: Shelley Manning – January 20, 2011 – 3:43 PM
To: Renee Greene
Subject: Re: Fwd: Reconsider?

You, judgmental? You are the least judgmental person I know. Now, if he were emailing Miss Priss, that would be different. (Sorry. Couldn't help it. I promise I'll be good tomorrow night.) Just ignore it. You don't want to get into a whole thing with this guy.

From: Renee Greene – January 20, 2011 – 3:54 PM
To: Shelley Manning
Subject: Re: Fwd: Reconsider?

Yes, please behave tomorrow. I just want to have a fun, peaceful evening. All right. I just won't respond to his message.

From: Ashley Price – January 21, 2011 – 4:01 PM
To: Shelley Manning
Cc: Renee Greene, Mark Finlay
Subject: Re: Renee's Birthday

Dinner at Alex's. Should be interesting based on all that I've heard about the place. I don't have any friends who have been there yet. Not really their type of place. But, should be fine. And of course, excited to celebrate Renee's birthday in style. She deserves it. Please make me a "plus one" as Evan is going to join us. Thanks.

From: Ashley Price – January 21, 2011 – 4:04 PM
To: Renee Greene
Subject: Re: Renee's Birthday

And I must say it is better than Pizza Party Zone. You know I love Mark, but what was he thinking? Like any of us would ever set foot into a restaurant that has a big frog as a mascot. Puh-lease!

And before you say anything, I talked to Evan and he promised that things would be different this time. He said he just got a bit scared because we were getting so serious. But he's really ready to commit.

I know, I know what you are going to say. But really, I mean where do you meet single men these days? Coffee houses have gotten so passé. A co-worker has been playing her hand at finding someone online. Can you imagine? How desperate must you be to resort to computer dating? How do you know that the man you are talking to really isn't some bored housewife in Tulsa or some teenager in Shreveport? On the Internet, no one is who they seem.

I know Evan isn't perfect. But I just know things will be better this time.

From: Renee Greene – January 21, 2011 – 5:15 PM
To: Shelley Manning
Subject: Fwd: Re: Renee's Birthday

This is why I don't want Ashley to know about my foray into the world of online dating. So, please, please PLEASE remember not to mention ANYTHING on Saturday night. I'll tell Mark the same.

From: Renee Greene – January 21, 2011 – 5:22 PM
To: Mark Finlay
Subject: Loose Lips

Hey there. Just a quick reminder not to mention anything about the online dating stuff at dinner on Saturday. Just want to keep this a little secret between you, me and Shelley. The rest of the world can find out on my wedding day ;)

From: Shelley Manning – January 22, 2011 – 9:30 AM
To: Renee Greene
Subject: Re: Fwd: Re: Renee's Birthday

No problem. Mum's the word. And what does Miss Priss mean that eligible men won't be at Alex's? It is only THE hottest restaurant in town. But, what would she know about what's in? I was so tempted to explain to Miss Priss that "Hollywood Chic" means no pearls, no skirts to the shin and no lace collars. However, leather dog collars are fine, even encouraged. How much do you want to bet she comes dressed like a nun on holiday?

From: Renee Greene – January 22, 2011 – 12:22 PM
To: Shelley Manning
Subject: Re: Fwd: Re: Renee's Birthday

Be nice! You know she's been my friend since grade school and although we are very different, she is a good person.

From: Mark Finlay – January 24, 2011 – 3:46 PM
To: Renee Greene
Subject: Re: Loose Lips

You got it. Not a word shall be uttered from my lips. See you at Shelley's place.

From: Shelley Manning – January 24, 2011 – 4:24 PM
To: Renee Greene
Subject: Re: Fwd: Re: Renee's Birthday

I will be on my best behavior. I promise. And if I don't, maybe Sister Priss, the Nun will crack my knuckles with a ruler. Okay, that was the last one. I promise. Mwah! Mwah!

From: meet@choosejews.com/OutdoorDude – January 25, 2011 – 6:03 PM
To: meet@choosejews.com/PRGal1981
Subject: Courtesy of a Response!

What, you think you're so high and mighty you don't even need to respond to an email? Well, I can tell you who you are. A snobby bitch. That's who.

From: Renee Greene – January 25, 2011 – 6:05 PM
To: Shelley Manning
Subject: Fwd: Courtesy of a Response!

All right. This is getting just a little freaky.

From: Shelley Manning – January 25, 2011 – 6:09 PM
To: Renee Greene
Subject: Re: Fwd: Courtesy of a Response!

Yikes. Talk about a psycho. Just ignore it.

From: meet@choosejews.com/OutdoorDude – January 28, 2011 – 9:03 AM
To: meet@choosejews.com/PRGal1981
Subject: SCREW YOU!

You cunt. You don't even give people the courtesy of responding.

From: Renee Greene – January 28, 2011 – 9:05 AM
To: Shelley Manning
Subject: Fwd: SCREW YOU!

What a way to celebrate my birthday. Okay, I'm printing out these emails and putting them in a folder in between my mattress and box spring. If anything suspicious ever happens to me, take them to the police. I'm serious. This is really starting to FUH-REAK ME OUT!

CHAPTER THREE – ANOTHER YEAR OLDER, ANOTHER YEAR WISER?

From: Renee Greene – January 29, 2011 – 11:36 AM
To: Shelley Manning
Subject: 30 Rocks!

Thank you! Thank you! I can't tell you what a pleasant experience turning 30 was. First of all, I GOT CARDED! Hurrah. Not a worry about turning 30 when the waiter thinks I'm 20. All I can say is thank goodness for fine line preventer. That stuff is the skin elixir of the gods.

Thank you also for my present. I love the earrings. All of the fashion magazines say chandelier earrings were the new big thing, so I'm glad to be in the midst of the fashion curve, rather than hopelessly behind, like I usually am.

I so appreciate all you did to make my day fun, special and pain free. You're the best.

From: Renee Greene – January 29, 2011 – 11:52 AM
To: Ashley Price
Subject: Thanks

Hey there. Just wanted to pop you a note to thank you again for coming out the other night for my birthday. It meant a lot that you were there. It's hard to believe we've been friends for 22 years. Who would have believed that Mrs. Brett's 3rd grade class would have turned out to be so worthwhile?

By the way, speaking of Mrs. Brett, I forgot to tell you that I bumped into Danny Newbridge the other day at the grocery store. He looks EXACTLY the same…just taller.

He's a lawyer now. Who would have guessed that someone who didn't do his "future city" project and failed third grade would have turned out okay? But I digress.

Thanks again for coming and thank you for the floral shawl. It's really lovely.

From: Renee Greene – January 29, 2011 – 11:58 AM
To: Mark Finlay
Subject: Pat-a-Cake, Pat-a-Cake, Baker's Woman!

I can't wait to start baking. Thanks so much for the basket of baking stuff...new sifter, measuring cups and spoons, cookbook, etc. I'm not sure if you got me all of this because you know I love to bake, or because you love to eat the fruits (or should I say cookies?) of my labor. Regardless, I really love it and know I will get a TON of use out of it all.

From: Mark Finlay – January 29, 2011 – 2:20 PM
To: Renee Greene
Subject: Re: Pat-a-Cake, Pat-a-Cake, Baker's Woman!

I'm so glad you like the basket. Now, I don't want to say I don't enjoy the – what did you call it? – fruits or cookies of your labor. You know I love your chocolate chip cookies. But I really wanted you to have something that you would enjoy and would use. I talked to both your parents and your sister to make sure I was getting the right kind of sifter and other "instruments." Happy baking!

From: Shelley Manning – January 31, 2011 – 9:06 AM
To: Renee Greene
Subject: Re: 30 Rocks!

I'm so glad you had a good time on Saturday. It was such a fun night and I knew the minute I saw those earrings, you had to have them. They'll look great with your hair pulled back. You deserve to be on the cutting edge. None of this talk about the tail end of fashion trends. Repeat after me…I AM A FASHION DIVA! I AM SUPERMODEL RENEE!

As far as this psycho is concerned, he doesn't know your name, address or phone number. He doesn't even know your real email address. Just ignore it.

From: Ashley Price – January 31, 2011 – 10:45 AM
To: Renee Greene
Subject: Re: Thanks

I'm so glad you like the shawl. I just figured it was something very classic and timeless that you could wear with a nice pair of slacks and a blouse, or a dress. I'm glad your birthday was a success. Crazy about Danny Newbridge. Would have NEVER guessed that he would amount to anything. Good for him. So, is he single? Married?

From: Renee Greene – January 31, 2011 – 11:58 AM
To: Ashley Price
Subject: Re: Thanks

He's married with two kids who look just like him, too. Weird.

From: Ashley Price – January 31, 2011 – 12:01 PM
To: Renee Greene
Subject: Re: Thanks

Of course he's married. Everyone has found someone except for me. Oh, did I mention that Evan and I broke up after your birthday dinner. I'm going to die an old maid.

From: Renee Greene – January 31, 2011 – 12:04 PM
To: Ashley Price
Subject: Re: Thanks

Hey now. Not everyone is married. I'm single. Shelley's single. Buck up! You will find someone and when you do, it will be special and wonderful and just what you deserve.

From: Ashley Price – January 31, 2011 – 12:14 PM
To: Renee Greene
Subject: Re: Thanks

Well, I'm not surprised Shelley's single. She seems to go through men like I go through – well I was going to make some rude analogy. But far be it from me to make a judgmental comment. Well, I wonder why you are single. You are such a kind and caring person. And, when you remember to get an eyebrow wax, your eyes totally pop. You'll find someone too. I'm certain of that. I have to go. Have a meeting with the boss.

From: meet@choosejews.com/CSUMD1008 – January 31, 2011 – 9:12 AM
To: meet@choosejews.com/PRGal1981
Subject: You seem interesting

Hi there. Loved your profile. I, too, like to sing off key in the car. But instead, I spend most of my time as a medical resident with a small hospital in Long Beach. My name is Brandon and I'm originally from Orange County. I just finished medical school in San Diego and started my residency in Long Beach. I should warn you that I do work some crazy hours (36 hour shifts!) and have to sleep at the hospital every fifth night (taking in ER admissions and delivering babies), but I am trying to balance work with a social life. Hoping you'll be intrigued enough by my profile and email back. Thanks.

From: Renee Greene – January 31, 2011 – 9:18 AM
To: Shelley Manning; Mark Finlay
Subject: Fwd: You seem interesting

Read below. Could it be? Have I hit the Jewish Mother trifecta – nice…Jewish…doctor?

From: Shelley Manning – January 31, 2011 – 10:22 AM
To: Renee Greene; Mark Finlay
Subject: Re: Fwd: You seem interesting

OMG! Your mom would be gushing right now if she knew about this! Go for it girl!

From: Mark Finlay – January 31, 2011 – 12:04 PM
To: Renee Greene; Shelley Manning
Subject: Re: Fwd: You seem interesting

MAJOR DITTO!

From: meet@choosejews.com/PRGal1981 – January 31, 2011 – 12:25 PM
To: meet@choosejews.com/CSUMD1008
Subject: Re: You seem interesting

Well, hi back. Wow! 36 hour shifts. Yikes! I can't imagine having to be coherent and on the ball for that many hours straight, especially when so much is riding on your work. It is impressive. I know you are a first year resident, but what is your specialization? What rotation are you on right now?

From: meet@choosejews.com/CSUMD1008 – January 31, 2011 – 7:06 PM
To: meet@choosejews.com/PRGal1981
Subject: Re: You seem interesting

It's not that impressive, trust me. Tons of people do it all the time. And, at night, as long as it's a bit quiet, I do manage to get a few hours of sleep. The worst is the waiting for the pager to go off. It's hard to fall asleep when you fear that someone is going to go into labor and wake you up. It pretty much sucks.

From: meet@choosejews.com/PRGal1981 – February 1, 2011 – 9:36 AM
To: meet@choosejews.com/CSUMD1008
Subject: Re: You seem interesting

Well, I'll keep my fingers crossed that there aren't any early morning deliveries. Although I must admit, it is a tad difficult to feel any sympathy for you, the doctor. I feel worse for the moms that are actually going through labor!

From: meet@choosejews.com/CSUMD1008 – February 1, 2011 – 2:45 PM
To: meet@choosejews.com/PRGal1981
Subject: Re: You seem interesting

No sympathy? Female solidarity, huh? Oh well. I guess I can see that. I was hoping that we could connect by phone – if that's okay with you. My number is (562) 555-3490. Call me.

From: meet@choosejews.com/CSUMD1008 – February 8, 2011 – 4:12 AM
To: meet@choosejews.com/PRGal1981
Subject: SO SORRY

So sorry I had to rush off the phone with your earlier. We had this crazy emergency. It was a case of priapism. What's priapism you might ask? Good question – although I hope you won't be offended by what I'm about to say.

You know those erectile dysfunction commercials where they say you should call your doctor if you have an erection that lasts more than 4 hours? Well, this 62-year-old man comes in with his "girlfriend" – which is code for hooker – and an erection that won't go down. He had to be rushed into surgery before he literally exploded. From a medical standpoint, it was fascinating and a great learning experience. From a general standpoint, it was hilarious!

So, I'm just getting back. Fortunately, my shift ends at 7:00. I figured I didn't want to sleep for a few hours because it will make it oh so much harder to fall asleep when I get home. And, I really don't know if I could sleep because I'm still in absolute shock that we went to the same Jewish sleep-away camp when we were kids. I'll have to dig up the old photos at my folks' place and show them to you so we can figure out if you're in any of them. Maybe this Monday night? I have the night off and was hoping to take you to dinner.

From: Renee Greene – February 8, 2011 – 9:18 AM
To: Shelley Manning
Subject: Fwd: SO SORRY

What the #$@%? Next Monday?!? Isn't that Valentine's Day? Is he seriously asking me out on a first date on Valentine's Day? This guy seems so smart, funny, interesting and normal. But this? This is three shades of crazy, no?

From: Shelley Manning – February 8, 2011 – 10:36 AM
To: Renee Greene
Subject: Re: Fwd: SO SORRY

He probably doesn't even realize it's V-day. He's a guy, after all. And a busy doctor on top of that.

Maybe he's just happy to have a night off and wants to spend it with a smart, beautiful, wonderful woman. Did you ever think of that, missy?

From: Renee Greene – February 8, 2011 – 12:22 PM
To: Shelley Manning
Subject: Re: Fwd: SO SORRY

Of course. You're probably right. Well, not about that last part, but about the part of him not realizing it's V-day. I'm going to email him back and tell him that it's V-day and I have plans to go to Tiffany's annual Blue Party but perhaps we can do it another time. Do you want me to bcc you?

From: Shelley Manning – February 8, 2011 – 12:25 PM
To: Renee Greene
Subject: Re: Fwd: SO SORRY

Hell ya!

From: meet@choosejews.com/PRGal1981 – February 8, 2011 – 12:36 PM
To: meet@choosejews.com/CSUMD1008
Bcc: Shelley Manning
Subject: Re: SO SORRY

I would love to meet for dinner. You probably don't realize it, but next Monday is Valentine's Day. Probably not the best night to go on a first date, huh? Anyway, I have my friend Tiffany's annual Blue Party where all of us singletons hang out, drink too much (then call in sick the next day!) and lament how "blue" we are that we don't have dates. So, when is your next free night?

From: meet@choosejews.com/CSUMD1008 – February 8, 2011 – 2:30 PM
To: meet@choosejews.com/PRGal1981
Bcc: Shelley Manning
Subject: Re: SO SORRY

Of course I know that next Monday is Valentine's Day. I asked for the night off so I could take you out. You don't need to be blue on Valentine's Day. You've got a date.

From: Renee Greene – February 8, 2011 – 2:35 PM
To: Shelley Manning
Subject: Fwd: Re: SO SORRY

Do you think it's weird that a guy wants to go on a first date on Valentine's Day? Isn't that a lot of pressure?

From: Shelley Manning – February 8, 2011 – 2:39 PM
To: Renee Greene
Subject: Re: Fwd: Re: SO SORRY

Yes. That's weird. Every guy I've ever met avoids V-Day like VD. In fact, I knew a guy who wouldn't date anyone between Thanksgiving and mid-February just so he wouldn't have to buy any Christmas or Valentine's gifts.

From: meet@choosejews.com/PRGal1981 – February 8, 2011 – 2:43 PM
To: meet@choosejews.com/CSUMD1008
Bcc: Shelley Manning
Subject: Re: SO SORRY

Brandon, that's really sweet, but I think I'd be more comfortable if we waited until after Valentine's Day. It's just a lot of pressure. I'm sure you understand.

From: meet@choosejews.com/CSUMD1008 – February 8, 2011 – 6:20 PM
To: meet@choosejews.com/PRGal1981
Bcc: Shelley Manning
Subject: Re: SO SORRY

I'm not feeling pressured at all. If anything, I feel like I've known you my whole life. I know this may sound strange, but I can really see there being a future between us.

From: Shelley Manning – February 8, 2011 – 6:32 PM
To: Renee Greene
Subject: Fwd: Re: SO SORRY

STALKER ALERT! STALKER ALERT! "Future between us"? He hasn't even met you yet, let alone seen you naked.

From: Renee Greene – February 8, 2011 – 6:41 PM
To: Shelley Manning
Subject: Re: Fwd: Re: SO SORRY

Yeah, this is WAY too much, too soon. Oh, and believe me, once they see me naked, they can't image a future WITH me.

From: Shelley Manning – February 8, 2011 – 6:45 PM
To: Renee Greene
Subject: Re: Fwd: Re: SO SORRY

Stop it right now. You know how I feel about you constantly putting yourself down. Now repeat after me, "I am a beautiful, smart, wonderful woman and any man would be lucky to see me naked." (You're a goddman supermodel for Christ sake!)

Do it. Do it! DO IT!!! I'm waiting…

From: Renee Greene – February 8, 2011 – 6:52 PM
To: Shelley Manning
Subject: Re: Fwd: Re: SO SORRY

I am a beautiful, smart, wonderful woman and any man would be lucky to see me naked.

Okay, back to the matter at hand. What do I say back?

From: Shelley Manning – February 8, 2011 – 8:12 PM
To: Renee Greene
Subject: Re: Fwd: Re: SO SORRY

Tell him you're feeling pressured and that this just isn't going to work out.

From: Renee Greene – February 8, 2011 – 8:14 PM
To: Shelley Manning
Subject: Re: Fwd: Re: SO SORRY

Do I need to call him or can I do it over email? As you well know, confrontation is not my strong suit.

From: Shelley Manning – February 8, 2011 – 8:17 PM
To: Renee Greene
Subject: Re: Fwd: Re: SO SORRY

Sorry sweetie, but I think you need to call him. If you hadn't spoken to him on the phone yet, an online kiss off would be fine. You can do this!

From: Renee Greene – February 8, 2011 – 8:20 PM
To: Shelley Manning
Subject: Re: Fwd: Re: SO SORRY

You're right, as usual. UGH! This is going to be painful. I'll let you know how it goes. In the meantime, going shopping tomorrow afternoon for a blue dress for Tiff's party.

From: Renee Greene – February 10, 2011 – 9:02 PM
To: Shelley Manning
Subject: Awkward Conversation!

Well, I *finally* got a hold of him. He really does work some insane hours. Let's just say, "Yikes!"

What an awkward conversation. Long story short (I know, a rarity for me!), I explained that *I* was the one feeling pressured and it's just a bit too much too soon. So, I thought it would be best if we just went our separate ways. He went on and on about how he always does this. He meets a great girl (which was weird because we haven't even met yet!) and gets too ahead of himself and scares her off. He just kept apologizing over and over and asking if I would reconsider. Maybe he and the Cuddler need to get together for a good cry. As for me, I'm diving into a can of frosting.

From: Shelley Manning – February 11, 2011 – 10:10 AM
To: Renee Greene
Subject: Re: Awkward Conversation!

I'm so proud of you, sweetie. You're really growing. (And don't make a crack about growing width-wise from the can of frosting. I know you were thinking that.) You really are making great strides toward becoming the confident woman I know you are. Kudos!

From: Renee Greene – February 11, 2011 – 10:12 AM
To: Shelley Manning
Subject: Re: Awkward Conversation!

Ha! The minute I read that I'm growing, of course the frosting and weight put-down came to mind. You really do know me so well! I'll see you Sunday.

From: Shelley Manning – February 15, 2011 – 10:36 AM
To: Renee Greene
Subject: What happened last night?!?

Hey there. Why aren't you answering your phone? Did you get lucky at Tiff's V-Day party? I sure did. Trouble is, I can't really remember anything after my third glass of her famous blue punch. I woke up at home – alone – but my face is all raw and blistery. Fill me in…please!

From: Renee Greene – February 15, 2011 – 10:52 AM
To: Shelley Manning
Subject: Re: What happened last night?!?

Morning, sunshine. Can't remember a thing, huh? Well, you had quite a night. Quite a night indeed.
As I recall, when I left around 1:00 a.m. (alone!), you were on a marathon make-out session with a young man who had a wee bit of stubble. I believe he shaved that morning as he usually does. But, that darn 5:00 shadow creeks up quickly. So, that basically means your face has rug burn.

From: Shelley Manning – February 15, 2011 – 11:05 AM
To: Renee Greene
Subject: Re: What happened last night?!?

Marathon make-out session, huh? Sounds like me. And who, pray tell, was my partner for this prolonged pecking? Was it that shaggy-haired guy from the creative department at her ad agency? Yum! The guy who just moved into her building with the shaved head? Yum! The guy with the tattoo of the bird on this arm? Extra Yum!

From: Renee Greene – February 15, 2011 – 11:06 AM
To: Shelley Manning
Subject: Re: What happened last night?!?

You really don't remember?

From: Shelley Manning – February 15, 2011 – 11:08 AM
To: Renee Greene
Subject: Re: What happened last night?!?

No. Should I be worried?

From: Renee Greene – February 15, 2011 – 11:09 AM
To: Shelley Manning
Subject: Re: What happened last night?!?

Are you sitting down?

From: Shelley Manning – February 15, 2011 – 11:10 AM
To: Renee Greene
Subject: Re: What happened last night?!?

Okay, you're starting to freak me out here. Just tell me.

From: Renee Greene – February 15, 2011 – 11:11 AM
To: Shelley Manning
Subject: Re: What happened last night?!?

It was Mark.

From: Shelley Manning – February 15, 2011 – 11:12 AM
To: Renee Greene
Subject: Re: What happened last night?!?

NO!!!!!!!!!!!!!!!!!!!!!!!!!!!!!! PLEASE, PLEASE TELL ME YOU ARE JOKING!!!!

From: Renee Greene – February 15, 2011 – 11:18 AM
To: Shelley Manning
Subject: Re: What happened last night?!?

I'm sorry. But it really was Mark.
You guys both got pretty bombed. Tiff's punch was a bit stronger than usual. He slipped a coaster under your drink, you yelled at him for being crazy and next thing we know, you two are going at it. And when I say going at it, I mean macking on each other like there was no tomorrow.

From: Shelley Manning – February 15, 2011 – 11:21 AM
To: Renee Greene
Subject: Re: What happened last night?!?

Oh God. Oh God. Me and Finlay. Did we sleep together? Dear God, please don't tell me we slept together!

From: Renee Greene – February 15, 2011 – 11:30 AM
To: Shelley Manning
Subject: Re: What happened last night?!?

No, you didn't sleep with him. According to Tiffany, he passed out and you got angry, called a cab and went home. If it's any consolation, he's a bit shaken up by your hook-up as well.

He called me this morning for a ride home from Tiffany's. That's where I was when you called and I couldn't very well talk to you while in the car with him. I'm "working from home" and emailing now instead of calling because he's in my bathroom tossing his cookies. Poor guy.

From: Shelley Manning – February 15, 2011 – 11:36 AM
To: Renee Greene
Subject: Re: What happened last night?!?

I feel like I'm going to toss my cookies. Not from having too much to drink, but from the thought of having hooked up with Finlay. Oh sweet lord. What the fuck was I thinking?

From: Renee Greene – February 15, 2011 – 11:38 AM
To: Shelley Manning
Subject: Re: What happened last night?!?

It happens to the best of us, my friend.

From: Shelley Manning – February 15, 2011 – 11:45 AM
To: Renee Greene
Subject: Re: What happened last night?!?

How will I ever face him again? Better yet, how can I ever face all of those people at the party who now know this shameful news? Most important, how can I look at myself in the mirror? Ugh! I'm going to take a shower and wash as much of this experience off of me as I can.

From: Renee Greene – February 15, 2011 – 11:51 AM
To: Shelley Manning
Subject: Re: What happened last night?!?

I'm sure it will all fade into the distance as an old memory. But, don't think I'll ever let you forget it. ;) Just kidding!

From: Ashley Price – February 15, 2011 – 2:03 PM
To: Renee Greene
Subject: What a spectacle!

Well, Shelley and Mark sure put on a show last night. It was quite the spectacle, wouldn't you say?

From: Renee Greene – February 15, 2011 – 3:10 PM
To: Ashley Price
Subject: Re: What a spectacle!

Yeah, it was something to say the least. I wouldn't bring it up to either of them, though. They are both a bit shaken up. Mark is embarrassed at having a drunken hook-up at a party. You know how he prides himself on his good manners. Knowing he was involved in a sloppy make-out session in front of 40+ people is really upsetting. And, Shelley is horrified because, well, no offense to him, it's Mark. ;)

From: Ashley Price – February 15, 2011 – 4:03 PM
To: Renee Greene
Subject: Re: What a spectacle!

Yeah, that was so not typical of Mark. I can see where he's feeling a bit uncomfortable.

But, I'm not surprised about Shelley. She's probably already worked her way through all of the men in Los Angeles and the only one left was Mark.

From: Renee Greene – February 15, 2011 – 4:10 PM
To: Ashley Price
Subject: Re: What a spectacle!

Be nice now.

So, did you meet anyone at the party? Do tell. Do tell.

From: Ashley Price – February 15, 2011 – 4:15 PM
To: Renee Greene
Subject: Re: What a spectacle!

Gosh no. Tiffany is great. I adore her. But, the guys she hangs with aren't really my type. Why can't I just meet a normal, successful, handsome man? I'm thinking of calling Evan. Don't judge.

From: Renee Greene – February 15, 2011 – 4:18 PM
To: Ashley Price
Subject: Re: What a spectacle!

You're preaching to the choir, my friend. Preaching to the choir. And regarding Evan, I'm not going to judge you. I just want you to be happy and if Evan makes you happy, then call him. But, I think you know deep down in your heart that he's not the right guy for you. If that's how you feel, you need to figure out a way to move on.

From: meet@choosejews.com/Stylin'Guy – February 15, 2011 – 9:40 PM
To: meet@choosejews.com/PRGal1981
Subject: You rock!

Hi. I'm Eric. Just read your profile and I think you are fabulous. Just FAB-U-LOUS.

I've always had a unique sense of style, which led me from my Midwestern upbringing to La-La land. After working as a costume designer for some small theatre companies, I landed an assistant gig on a short-lived TV show.
But, that's where I met my mentor who helped me get my current job as wardrobe stylist on "Family Days." Despite the fact that shopping is a major part of my job, I could – as they say – shop 'til I drop.

In my free time, I hang out with friends, attend the theatre, concerts and nightclubs and love to cook. In fact, we have an amazing amount in common based on your profile – interests, hobbies and personality traits. Check mine out and maybe we can chat.

From: Renee Greene – February 16, 2011 – 9:32 AM
To: Shelley Manning
Subject: Fwd: You rock!

Just got an email from this guy and read his profile. He seems great and normal. We do seem to have a lot in common. Thoughts?

From: Shelley Manning – February 16, 2011 – 1:02 PM
To: Renee Greene
Subject: Re: Fwd: You rock!

Wow! You really do have a lot in common. And, he's a wardrobe stylist. I hear those guys have tons of things left over from the set…shoes, handbags, jewelry. You never know. Maybe you'll get some "Family Days" leftovers. And his photo is really cute.

From: Renee Greene – February 17, 2011 – 3:00 PM
To: Shelley Manning
Subject: Re: Fwd: You rock!

Never really thought about the wardrobe stuff, but good point. I'm just worried that he's going to scrutinize what I'm wearing. Am I hip enough for a wardrobe stylist? Okay, first things first. I'll email him back. I put together a short list of questions to help me weed through all of these gentleman callers after my initial three online introductions went awry – one out-of-towner, one psycho and one desperado doctor. I'll bcc you.

From: meet@choosejews.com/PRGal1981 – February 17, 2011 – 5:05 PM
To: meet@choosejews.com/Stylin'Guy
Bcc: Shelley Manning
Subject: Re: Inquiring Minds Want to Know

Eric, thanks so much for your email. I read your profile and I think you are right, we do have a lot in common including a strong love of the theatre and shopping. So, let me ask you a few questions:

- Who is your favorite Brady?

- If Bionic Woman and Wonder Woman got in a fight, who would win?
- What is the last book you read or are currently reading?
- What is the best part of being a costume designer for "Family Days"?

Looking forward to hearing back from you.

Renee

From: Shelley Manning – February 17, 2011 – 5:15 PM
To: Renee Greene
Subject: Fwd: Re: Inquiring Minds Want to Know

Hilarious! Cracked up at the Wonder Woman/Bionic Woman question. Can't wait to see the responses.

From: meet@choosejews.com/Stylin'Guy – February 18, 2011 – 9:50 AM
To: meet@choosejews.com/PRGal1981
Bcc: Shelley Manning
Subject: Re: Inquiring Minds Want to Know

Love the questions. Love 'em. Here are some quick responses:

Favorite Brady – Peter. I just love that episode where Mom said "Don't play ball in the house" and Peter learned the valuable lesson of telling the truth. I'm a big believer in the truth.

Wonder Woman would win hands down. She had the most fab, patriotic outfit and that golden lasso that made people tell the truth. Gold bangle bracelets that thwarted bullets and the invisible jet. She truly was a force to be reckoned with.

Right now, I'm reading a biography on Lady Gaga. I didn't realize what a philanthropist she is.

The best part of my job is transforming those little tarts into the sweet and innocent characters they appear to be on screen.

Listen, I know this is going to sound crazy and I'm not trying to rush you, but I'm supposed to see "My Fair Lady" tomorrow night at the Pantages and my friend just canceled. Was wondering if you wanted to go?

From: Renee Greene – February 18, 2011 – 10:46 AM
To: Shelley Manning
Subject: Take the Plunge?

Eric wants to take me to see "My Fair Lady" tomorrow night. What do you think? Should I go? Is it too soon? How do I know he's not an ax murderer?

From: Shelley Manning – February 18, 2011 – 11:05 AM
To: Renee Greene
Subject: Re: Take the Plunge?

I know! I'm getting Bcc'd on all. This is SO FUN! Hell ya you should go. A ticket to see "My Fair Lady." It's starring Harry Connick, Jr. and Lea Michele. It's sold out until September. Besides, you might get lucky. He sounds hot. Just be careful and meet him at the theater. That way he doesn't know where you live.

From: meet@choosejews.com/PRGal1981 – February 18, 2011 – 11:36 AM
To: meet@choosejews.com/Stylin'Guy
Bcc: Shelley Manning
Subject: Re: Inquiring Minds Want to Know

Sounds great. I'll come straight from work, so why don't I just meet you at the theatre. I know your picture is on the site, but it will likely be crowded. How will I find you? Also, what's your last name?

From: meet@choosejews.com/Stylin'Guy – February 18, 2011 – 2:25PM
To: meet@choosejews.com/PRGal1981
Bcc: Shelley Manning
Subject: Re: Inquiring Minds Want to Know

Oh, I understand. Don't want some strange man picking you up. I don't blame you. There are a lot of nut jobs out there today. I'll be wearing a black D&G suit with a powder blue shirt. And, it's Rosen. Eric Rosen. Wow! That sounded so Bond, James Bond.

From: meet@choosejews.com/PRGal1981 – February 18, 2011 – 2:32 PM
To: meet@choosejews.com/Stylin'Guy
Bcc: Shelley Manning
Subject: Re: Inquiring Minds Want to Know

I'm really looking forward to it. See you tomorrow.

From: Renee Greene – February 18, 2011 – 2:40 PM
To: Shelley Manning, Mark Finlay
Subject: It's a Go!

Okay. I'm going for it. My first foray into online dating. His name is Eric Rosen. He is a costume designer for "Family Days." The show is at the Pantages Theatre. I'll call you as soon as I get home. If you don't hear from me by 11:30, call the police. I'll have last been seen in tan suede pants, black leather boots, a black turtleneck sweater and my new chandelier earrings. Is that okay to wear on a date with a stylist?

From: Shelley Manning – February 18, 2011 – 2:56 PM
To: Renee Greene
Subject: Re: It's a Go!

Will keep your wardrobe description on hand in case an all-points bulletin is needed. I'm sure you are going to be fine. You're going to a very public place. Have a GREAT time. And don't worry about your outfit. I've seen those suede pants. Very hot…very cool. You're gonna look great. ALERT! PETTY ALERT! You mean you're not wearing that matronly flower thing Miss Priss bought you. END ALERT. Can't wait to hear all about your date. Mwah! Mwah!

From: Mark Finlay – February 18, 2011 – 2:40 PM
To: Renee Greene
Subject: Re: It's a Go!

So excited for you. Can't wait to hear all about it. Have fun but be safe and call me when you get home. Doesn't matter what time it is. I'll be up.

From: Renee Greene – February 19, 2011 – 11:46 PM
To: Shelley Manning
Subject: Safe and Sound

Just left you a message (by the way – where are you at 11:30 on a school night?), but didn't want to leave all of this on your answering machine. I'm home, safe and sound. Nothing to worry about here. Eric is gay.
Now Eric doesn't yet know he is gay. But, he is undoubtedly, unremarkably, without question…quite gay. How do I know? A few clues tipped me off. 1) He's a very snappy dresser. Not that it should have surprised me. He is a wardrobe stylist after all. But, he looked too sharp. Know what I mean? When he described his outfit as a D&G suit, I should have guessed. But after seeing him, it became decidedly clear. 2) He couldn't stop staring at this very hot usher who was taking equal interest in him. 3) He cried – yes CRIED – during the show. UGH! I'm going to bed now. Online dating in LA is no different than regular dating in LA. All of the good guys want the other good guys. <sigh>

From: meet@choosejews.com/Stylin'Guy – February 20, 2011 – 9:03 AM
To: meet@choosejews.com/PRGal1981
Subject: I could have danced all night!

What a glorious morning. I awoke with such a song in my heart. Not only was the play last night just fabulous, but I think you are fabulous too. I had a marvelous time and would love to take you out again. Joel, the key make-up artist on the show is having a small soiree at his place next Saturday. It will be an evening with great wine and even better conversation. Interested?

From: meet@choosejews.com/PRGal1981 – February 20, 2011 – 10:30 AM
To: meet@choosejews.com/Stylin'Guy
Subject: Re: I could have danced all night!

Eric: I had such a great time last night. You are really a terrific guy. But, I'm just not feeling that love connection. I'm so sorry. I would really love to spend time with you as a friend, but I honestly don't see it going beyond that. I'll understand if you aren't interested in getting together again.

---

meet@choosejews.com/Stylin'Guy – February 20, 2011 – 10:45 AM
To: meet@choosejews.com/PRGal1981
Subject: Re: I could have danced all night!

Is this because I cried during the show? A lot of men cry you know.

From: meet@choosejews.com/PRGal1981 – February 20, 2011 – 10:48 AM
To: meet@choosejews.com/Stylin'Guy
Subject: Re: I could have danced all night!

No, of course not. I enjoy a man who is in touch with his emotions. It's not something I can really explain. You just kind of know it. I'm really sorry.

From: meet@choosejews.com/PureFun43 – February 24, 2011 – 8:46 AM
To: meet@choosejews.com/PRGal1981
Subject: Looking for Love?

Hi there. I'm an energetic and friendly chiropractor looking for love in Los Angeles. My interests range from a to z – literally – from art to zen studies. I'm a romantic at heart who loves long walks on the beach and candle lit dinners (which if you cook, I will gladly clean up after). But, I'm also outdoorsy and active, having played water polo in college and bike riding about 15+ miles a day.

I believe that honesty and respect are the cornerstones of a good relationship. Without trust to share all of your thoughts and feelings, we can't truly be committed to one another.

Please take a look at my profile and let me know if you're interested in meeting.

P.S. You should know, that I practice abstinence before marriage. I know it sounds a bit corny or old fashioned, but I believe that pledging yourself to life with another person should include giving yourself completely to them and only them. So, I've been willing to wait for the right person to come along.

From: Renee Greene – February 24, 2011 – 10:02 AM
To: Shelley Manning
Subject: Fwd: Looking for Love?

OH! EM! GEE! OMG! OMG! OMG!

Read through the email below but <u>DO NOT READ</u> the "P.S." Don't cheat! Trust me! This will be good.

Okay, you've read through the profile? This man looks perfect – perfect! – on paper. He seems honest, interesting, successful, active, romantic, etc. Right?

Okay, now read the "P.S."

And go! (This oughta be good.)

From: Shelley Manning – February 24, 2011 – 11:06 AM
To: Renee Greene
Subject: Re: Fwd: Looking for Love?

Wow. I feel like I just ate a frozen yogurt and I have that horrible brain freeze feeling. My head hurts.

On one hand, I'm just speechless – which is such a rarity, I know.

On the other hand, SAY WHAT?!? The flood gates have opened so quickly. Can't…type…too…many… thoughts…spilling out…brain…on….overload…

From: Renee Greene – February 24, 2011 – 11:09 AM
To: Shelley Manning
Subject: Re: Fwd: Looking for Love?

So, what should I do?

From: Shelley Manning – February 24, 2011 – 11:11 AM
To: Renee Greene
Subject: Re: Fwd: Looking for Love?

Well, you're not thinking about going out with him, are you?

From: Renee Greene – February 24, 2011 – 11:15 AM
To: Shelley Manning
Subject: Re: Fwd: Looking for Love?

Hell no! It's not like I've been with a lot of men (no offense to you), but I've been with a few. And, I've been around enough, read enough and talked with girlfriends enough to know that you've got to make sure the goods are good. Don't you agree?

From: Shelley Manning – February 24, 2011 – 11:26 AM
To: Renee Greene
Subject: Re: Fwd: Looking for Love?

First off, no offense taken. And, I'm totally with you. When making sure someone's got the whole package, you got to check out the "package" among other things. Sexual compatibility is VERY important. So important, in fact, I've based several reasonably long relationships on that factor alone. ;)

From: Renee Greene – February 24, 2011 – 11:37 AM
To: Shelley Manning
Subject: Re: Fwd: Looking for Love?

Okay, so what do I do now? Ignore it? Email back and tell him thanks, but no thanks? Guidance, oh wise one.

From: Shelley Manning – February 24, 2011 – 11:40 AM
To: Renee Greene
Subject: Re: Fwd: Looking for Love?

I say ignore it. For all he knows, you're getting 15-20 emails a day and just can't be bothered to respond to all.

From: Renee Greene – February 24, 2011 – 11:52 AM
To: Shelley Manning
Subject: Re: Fwd: Looking for Love?

You don't think that's rude? You know how I hate to be rude. And remember what nonsense ensued the last time I ignored an email?

From: Shelley Manning – February 24, 2011 – 11:54 AM
To: Renee Greene
Subject: Re: Fwd: Looking for Love?

Yes, Miss Manners. I know how you are. And yes, I remember the psycho. But seriously, in this case, I think it's much nicer to ignore it than tell him he's a 35-year-old freak of nature.

From: Renee Greene – February 24, 2011 – 11:59 AM
To: Shelley Manning
Subject: Re: Fwd: Looking for Love?

You have a point. Thanks. Well, the search continues. Onward!

From: meet@choosejews.com/TheLAWay – February 27, 2011 – 5:56 PM
To: meet@choosejews.com/PRGal1981
Subject: A lot in common

Hi there. Was reading through your profile and you seem really down-to-earth and fun. I think we have a lot in common. We're even the same sign. Not that I'm one of those cheesy guys who want to know what sign you are. That is so Larry from "Three's Company."

I'm an actor in Los Angeles – host of "Forensic Mystery TV" – who is looking to get beyond the superficiality and quid pro quo of the Hollywood scene. I'm looking to meet a great gal who is more interested in me as a person than who I know and how it can help her career. I pride myself on being a sensitive and caring person and expect the same from my girlfriend. But, my job can be very demanding, so I'm looking for someone who is flexible and understanding.

Anyway, check out my profile and write back.

Davey

From: meet@choosejews.com/PRGal1981 – February 28, 2011 – 9:32 AM
To: meet@choosejews.com/TheLAWay
Subject: Re: A lot in common

Hi Davey. Thanks so much for your note. I've seen the show and am a big fan.

So, let me ask you a few questions:

- Who is your favorite Brady?

- If Bionic Woman and Wonder Woman got in a fight, who would win?
- What is the last book you read or are currently reading?
- What is the best part of being on television?

Looking forward to hearing back from you.

From: meet@choosejews.com/TheLAWay – February 28, 2011 – 2:00 PM
To: meet@choosejews.com/PRGal1981
Subject: Re: A lot in common

My favorite Brady – Marcia, Marcia Marcia =)

Bionic Woman vs. Wonder Woman – hands down the Bionic Woman…she cost millions to make and Wonder Woman carries around a cheap gold lamé rope.

Last book – Biography of Henry Ford. I'm working on a bio pic about his life right now.

Best part of being a TV star – It's really just being there for the fans. It's hard to explain, but just knowing that I'm bringing entertainment and joy into people's living rooms and lives really means a lot.

From: Renee Greene – February 28, 2011 – 3:30 PM
To: Shelley Manning
Subject: You WON'T believe it!!!

You won't believe who I've been emailing…Davey Montrell from "Forensic Mystery TV." He is so charming. Do you think I should go out with him? I've always shied away from the Hollywood scene.

From: Shelley Manning – February 28, 2011 – 4:02 PM
To: Renee Greene
Subject: Re: You WON'T believe it!!!

Absolutely. He's got great hair. But, everyone in LA is someone or wants to be someone. Don't be intimated. You…are Supermodel Renee!!!!

From: Renee Greene – February 28, 2011 – 4:08 PM
To: Shelley Manning
Subject: Re: You WON'T believe it!!!

Where do you think he would take me? Somewhere totally expensive and very LA?

From: Shelley Manning – February 28, 2011 – 4:10 PM
To: Renee Greene
Subject: Re: You WON'T believe it!!!

Stop emailing me and email him. Won't get anywhere talking with me…

From: meet@choosejews.com/PRGal1981 – February 28, 2011 – 4:12 PM
To: meet@choosejews.com/TheLAWay
Subject: Re: A lot in common

Henry Ford. How exciting. I bet playing Henry Ford is a great role. He seemed like such an interesting, inventive and visionary person. When and where do you start filming?

From: meet@choosejews.com/TheLAWay – March 1, 2011 – 8:07 AM
To: meet@choosejews.com/PRGal1981
Subject: Re: A lot in common

Oh, I wouldn't want to play Ford. I'm much more interested in Harold Miller, he was one of Ford's neighbors when he was a boy and inadvertently inspired him to invent. There's this really pivotal scene in the beginning of the movie that really sets up the rest of the story about Ford's life. A part like that is much more interesting and challenging. You know, when it's not all there on the page. You've really got to delve deep into the character and his motivation. But, it would probably be much better to explain all of this in person. Are you up for meeting?

From: meet@choosejews.com/PRGal1981 – March 1, 2011 – 10:02 AM
To: meet@choosejews.com/TheLAWay
Subject: Re: A lot in common

Sure thing. What did you have in mind?

From: meet@choosejews.com/TheLAWay – March 1, 2011 – 12:26 PM
To: meet@choosejews.com/PRGal1981
Subject: Re: A lot in common

Why don't I pick you up around 8:30 on Saturday night? We'll go grab a bite and see where the night takes us.

From: meet@choosejews.com/PRGal1981 – March 1, 2011 – 12:35 PM
To: meet@choosejews.com/TheLAWay
Subject: Re: A lot in common

Sounds great. I'm at the southwest corner of Pico and Beverly Glen, #402. I'll see you then.

From: Renee Greene – March 1, 2011 – 12:38 PM
To: Shelley Manning
Subject: Mrs. Davey Montrell

AGH! HE ASKED ME OUT…I CAN'T WAIT. Can't you just picture me, Mrs. Davey Montrell. We'd be at all of the parties. I'm going out with HIM. We're going to "grab a bite and see where the night takes us."

From: Shelley Manning – March 1, 2011 – 1:05 PM
To: Renee Greene
Subject: Re: Mrs. Davey Montrell

I'm more impressed that Davey Montrell is going out with RENEE GREENE! I'm her biggest fan – but not in a stalkerish kind of way. ;)

From: Renee Greene – March 1, 2011 – 2:15 PM
To: Mark Finlay
Subject: Just call me…Mrs. Davey Montrell

Yes, you read correctly. I have the potential to become Mrs. Davey Montrell. He emailed me and asked me out on a date. We're going out on Saturday night. If this works out, I owe you – BIG TIME.

From: Mark Finlay – March 1, 2011 – 3:45 PM
To: Renee Greene
Subject: Re: Just call me…Mrs. Davey Montrell

Awesome. Not only could you be hob nobbing with all of the celeb types, but you'll owe me. Have fun – be safe!!! And, make sure you call or email when you get home.

From: Renee Greene – March 2, 2011 – 10:14 AM
To: Ashley Price
Subject: Set up?

Hey there. Since your (thankfully!) recent break up (again!) with Evan, I haven't heard you talk much about dating anyone. Was wondering if you would let me set you up with someone? We have a sister agency called Foxmeade and I recently met a managing director named Austin who is TOTALLY awesome. Now you may be asking yourself, why doesn't Renee go out with him herself? Well, I would absolutely consider it, but I NEVER mix work with pleasure and we will be working together on a few projects. So, you're thinking, "well, what's he like?" He's very savvy, creative and engaging. Next, you may be asking yourself, "so what does this guy with a 'great personality' look like?" He's very tall and quite handsome with dark brown hair, warm brown eyes and a really gentle smile. That leads you right to "If he's so great, why is he single," right? Good question. He was in a serious relationship and his girlfriend got an amazing job offer in Europe. They tried the long distance thing, but it was just too hard. He's been on his own for about four months. So, I thought to myself, "who is a charming, successful, beautiful and smart woman who would be worthy of such a fine man" and you IMMEDIATELY sprung to mind. So, what do you think? Up for it?

From: Ashley Price – March 2, 2011 – 10:19 AM
To: Renee Greene
Subject: Re: Set up?

Well, you certainly know how to sell something. Your clients are VERY lucky. And you certainly know how to flatter a girl. But, really, I don't know.

From: Renee Greene – March 2, 2011 – 10:22 AM
To: Ashley Price
Subject: Re: Set up?

Oh, come on. What have you got to lose? It's one night and I vouch for him. He's a really good guy. He mentioned that one of their partners' clients is hosting a big party to launch a new casino in Palm Springs. It's a casino-themed event in Hollywood and supposedly some celebrities will be there. He needs a date. Say yes!?!

From: Ashley Price – March 2, 2011 – 3:00 PM
To: Renee Greene
Subject: Re: Set up?

Agh!!!!!!!!!!!!!!!!!!

Okay. I'm in. Give him my number.

From: Renee Greene – March 2, 2011 – 3:01 PM
To: Ashley Price
Subject: Re: Set up?

:)

From: Renee Greene – March 5, 2011 – 11:55 PM
To: Shelley Manning
Subject: He is a small, small man

When I say small, I mean small in every sense of the word. First, this man is not the 5'8" he claims to be in his profile. No, he's lucky if he cracks the 5'3" barrier. Not that I'm judging. I'm short. So height has never really been a huge relationship factor for me. But 5'8"? No way. Even more important, he is a small-minded, petty, rude, little man. I would say he has a Napoleon complex, but he couldn't get a part as "big" as Napoleon. And as he would justify it, he would much rather delve into a smaller character so "it's not all there on the page."

So, we're sitting at dinner (he took me to The Red Room) and over walks this couple who look very Hollywood. He's middle-age, balding with a round belly and she looks like her parents let her stay out late on a school night…a collagen-lipped, silicone-injected, bleach blonde-headed bimbo doll. He stands up, gives a few air kisses and proceeds to chat for 10 minutes. Believe it or not, the phrase "do lunch" was actually uttered. Now normally, I wouldn't mind. I love to chat with new people and can hold my own among any crowd.

But the man DIDN'T EVEN INTRODUCE ME. It was like I wasn't even there. After they left, he proceeds to tell me what phonies they are and that he didn't introduce me because they have no interest in "the little people." Here he is saying how much he wants to find someone beyond the superficiality, but in reality, he is the biggest phony of them all.

Then, he sees a man a few tables away – of course he's sitting at the table Davey wanted but was too cheap to slip a few bucks to the maître d – and spends a HALF HOUR telling me what an ass he is, how he stole a part from him, etc. Not once did he ever ask me a question about myself and every time I started to talk about my life, interests, etc. he managed to turn the conversation back to his career and fans. UGH!

Gotta run and call Mark.

From: Shelley Manning – March 7, 2011 – 8:56 AM
To: Renee Greene
Subject: Re: He is a small, small man

Sorry I'm just getting back to you. What a lame ass. They say the camera adds 10 pounds. Maybe he thought he could add it length wise instead of width wise. Wow. So sorry. Obviously you aren't going out with him again. How did the date end?

As for me, I spent a weekend-long date in a sweat-soaked set of satin sheets. His name was Charlie and we met through a mutual friend. Now granted, we were being quite aerobic, but this man was sweating – profusely. Thankfully, it was an attractive, musky, manly scent that protruded from his highly-active pores. From now on, he will be known as Fire Hose. And, ironically, that also helps to describe another manly feature of his. :)

From: Renee Greene – March 7, 2011 – 9:14 AM
To: Shelley Manning
Subject: Re: He is a small, small man

Believe it or not, he actually seemed shocked that I didn't want to invite him in and have sex with him. What on earth would make him think that was in the cards? I'm just going to email him and call it off. Too bad I'm not very "Hollywood" or I could have my people call his people. But, when you are one of the "little people," you gotta take care of dirty business yourself.

And, as far as Fire Hose is concerned, gotta say, EW! I'm not big into the sweat. But, at least he was a man – not like the Cuddler. I bet when he sweats, it's like jasmine, lilacs and perfume. ;).

From: meet@choosejews.com/PRGal1981 – March 7, 2011 – 9:28 AM
To: meet@choosejews.com/TheLAWay
Subject: Thanks

Thanks for dinner last night. It was fun…but I think we make better friends than anything. Hope you understand.

From: meet@choosejews.com/TheLAWay – March 7, 2011 – 9:35 AM
To: meet@choosejews.com/PRGal1981
Subject: Re: Thanks

I was just about to email you. You seem like a nice person, but quite frankly I'm looking for someone who is a little more outgoing and dynamic. Sadly, in my business, it's all about image and I just don't see you fitting into mine.

From: Renee Greene – March 7, 2011 – 9:37 AM
To: Shelley Manning
Subject: Fwd: Re: Thanks

Can you believe I'm getting dumped by this ass?

From: Shelley Manning – March 7, 2011 – 10:05 AM
To: Renee Greene
Subject: Re: Fwd: Re: Thanks

What a jerk. You deserve much better than this B-list celebrity. He's not EVEN worth getting upset over. He would be LUCKY to be going out with someone like you. Lucky, I tell you. We should take his lame emails and sell them to the tabloids.

From: meet@choosejews.com/Thomas33 – March 7, 2011 – 10:07 AM
To: meet@choosejews.com/PRGal1981
Subject: Hello

Hi. I'm a junior partner for Hastings, Laslow, Arden and Stein, a large law firm in downtown Los Angeles I went to college at UCLA and got my joint MBA/JD from Wharton. My parents have been married for 36 years and are great relationship role models for me. My dad worked hard to provide for his family and my mom was the family caretaker. I hope to find the same kind of relationship. Take a look at my profile and let me know if you think you would like to talk with me. Thanks, Thomas.

From: meet@choosejews.com/PRGal1981 – March 8, 2011 – 9:36 AM
To: meet@choosejews.com/Thomas33
Subject: Re: Hello

Hi Tom. You seem like a very smart, ambitious and interesting guy. So, let me ask you a few questions.

- Who is your favorite Brady?
- If Bionic Woman and Wonder Woman got in a fight, who would win?
- What is the last book you read or are currently reading?
- What is the best part of being an attorney?

Looking forward to hearing back from you.

From: Renee Greene – March 8, 2011 – 9:45 AM
To: Ashley Price
Subject: Up-DATE?

So, what's the update on your date? Did you have fun? Was he as advertised? Are you going to see him again?

From: Ashley Price – March 8, 2011 – 10:32 AM
To: Renee Greene
Subject: Re: Up-DATE?

It was fine. The party was okay – a bit too crowded to play any of the casino games and the food was mediocre. But, I got a GREAT gift bag including a gift certificate for $500 (!) worth of services at swanky Ra Jai salon in Beverly Hills. And, you were right. Austin is a very nice, charming and handsome guy. Completely as advertised.

From: Renee Greene – March 8, 2011 – 11:01 AM
To: Ashley Price
Subject: Re: Up-DATE?

So, are you going to see him again?

From: Ashley Price – March 8, 2011 – 11:48 AM
To: Renee Greene
Subject: Re: Up-DATE?

Please don't be angry with me. But, I couldn't stop thinking about Evan. I know he was a jerk and I know I'm better off without him, but I couldn't help myself but miss being with him. I'm sorry.

From: Renee Greene – March 8, 2011 – 11:57 AM
To: Ashley Price
Subject: Re: Up-DATE?

Oh Ashley! With one hand, he's giving you a big caress. He keeps telling you that he loves you and wants to be with you. And with the other hand, he's giving you a big ol' slap in the face. He doesn't think he can commit to you…or anyone for that matter. You guys break up and then he calls or texts or stops by to see you and you're back together. But, if he doesn't see a future with you, you need to move on. Again, the most important thing is for you to be happy and I just don't see you happy. I have to hop into a meeting. I'll call you tonight.

From: meet@choosejews.com/Thomas33 – March 8, 2011 – 10:17 AM
To: meet@choosejews.com/PRGal1981
Subject: Re: Hello

Actually, I prefer Thomas. To answer your questions:

- Who is your favorite Brady? I guess the dad
- If Bionic Woman and Wonder Woman got in a fight, who would win? Don't really know
- What is the last book you read or are currently reading? Intellectual Property Rights in the Digital Era, Second Edition by Joe I. Bessis. Sadly, I don't have much time to read for pleasure.
- What is the best part of being an attorney? Working for one of the world's leading firms.

Listen, I'm not very good at this online thing. Would you be interested in meeting me for a drink at the Coffee World in Brentwood? Do you know where that is?

From: meet@choosejews.com/PRGal1981 – March 9, 2011 – 9:13 AM
To: meet@choosejews.com/Thomas33
Subject: Re: Hello

I know exactly where that is. Sure. That would be nice. Why don't we say Thursday night around 8:00. Let's plan to meet outside.

From: meet@choosejews.com/Thomas33 – March 9, 2011 – 9:15 AM
To: meet@choosejews.com/PRGal1981
Subject: Re: Hello

Sounds good. See you then.

From: Renee Greene – March 9, 2011 – 9:17 AM
To: Shelley Manning; Mark Finlay
Subject: Third time's the charm

Okay, Date #3. His name is Thomas (not Tom, but Thomas) Wells and he is a junior partner with Hastings, Laslow, Arden and Stein. We're meeting at Coffee World tomorrow. Wish me luck.

From: Shelley Manning – March 9, 2011 – 9:20 AM
To: Renee Greene, Mark Finlay
Subject: Re: Third time's the charm

Junior partner, eh? Can you say CHA-CHING? Have fun and call me or drop me an email when you're home.

From: Mark Finlay – March 9, 2011 – 9:20 AM
To: Renee Greene; Shelley Manning
Subject: Re: Third time's the charm

Ditto for me. Not the "CHA-CHING" part, but the "have fun and call me later" part.

From: Renee Greene – March 10, 2011 – 10:15 PM
To: Ashley Price
Subject: THANK YOU!

THANK YOU! THANK YOU! THANK YOU! I cannot thank you enough for bailing me out. That man was probably the most boring person I have EVER met in my entire life. And I've been around. Well, I haven't actually been around in that sense. But, you know what I mean. I've met a lot of people and lord knows I've got some clients that could put you to sleep, but this man takes the cake. I've never done anything like that before, but thank goodness you were home.

From: Renee Greene – March 10, 2011 – 10:20 PM
To: Shelley Manning; Mark Finlay
Subject: Safe, sound, sleepy

Holy moly. Thomas was probably the MOST BORING PERSON EVER! That lemonade (sadly, at Coffee World so no vanilla blended to take my mind off of this bore) felt like a valium cocktail with an ambien chaser. I could not keep my eyes open. Guess my search continues. Call me tomorrow.

From: Ashley Price – March 11, 2011 – 9:06 AM
To: Renee Greene
Subject: Re: THANK YOU!

Happy to oblige. Evan and I were just hanging out watching a movie. So, who was this guy and how did you meet?

From: Renee Greene – March 11, 2011 – 9:08 AM
To: Ashley Price
Subject: Re: THANK YOU!

He is a junior partner with some big law firm downtown.

From: Ashley Price – March 11, 2011 – 10:15 AM
To: Renee Greene
Subject: Re: THANK YOU!

A junior partner?!? Wow! How did you meet him? Was it a set-up? It's not like your job brings you in touch with that kind of man.

From: Renee Greene – March 11, 2011 – 11:45 AM
To: Ashley Price
Subject: Re: THANK YOU!

Yep. Set up through a friend at work. She knows someone who knows him. My god was he boring. He was like the Ambien of the dating world. If I ever have insomnia, I can just relive moments over a vanilla blended where he droned on and on about intellectual property rights. Sorry. I'm probably putting you to sleep right now just giving you the highlights – or low lights in this case. Anyway, thanks again. You are a real pal.

From: Ashley Price – March 11, 2011 – 11:50 PM
To: Renee Greene
Subject: Re: THANK YOU!

Anytime. That's what friends are for.

From: Renee Greene – March 11, 2011 – 12:20 PM
To: Shelley Manning
Subject: Three strikes and you're out?

Last night was the most boring evening of my life. The absolute worst date I've ever – EVER – been on and that even includes the guy who stole my wallet. I had to excuse myself, go to the ladies room, call Ashley and have her page me with some fake emergency so I could get out of it. I'm starting to think this online dating thing just isn't for me. So far, I've dated a gay man, an egomaniacal B celebrity and the most boring man on the planet. What made me think quality men would be searching for love on the net? <sigh>

From: Shelley Manning – March 14, 2011 – 1:45 PM
To: Renee Greene
Subject: Re: Three strikes and you're out?

I've resorted to the fake emergency before, but not from boredom. You know me. I don't care if they're boring, as long as they're hot. So, was he hot? Can I have his number? HA! I knew that would make you smile. Don't give up. Three dates is nothing. I sometimes go on three dates in one day. Knew that would make you laugh, too. You just need to hang in there. Lunch at Mel's on Wednesday?

From: Renee Greene – March 14, 2011 – 2:20 PM
To: Shelley Manning
Subject: Re: Three strikes and you're out?

Lunch sounds great. Will call Ashley and let her know.

From: Mark Finlay – March 14, 2011 – 11:05 PM
To: Renee Greene
Subject: My Profile for Review

Finally! My profile is – almost – complete. I've written it and gotten feedback from my sister…and your sister (LOL!). Now it's time for me to get feedback from the ultimate writing czar and grammar hawk. Having a friend in PR sure comes in handy. Hoping you will take a look, make suggestions, check for typos, etc.

If you're looking for an accomplished and driven, self made man, I could be the right match for you. My name is Mark and I'm a 29 year old video game designer. I used to work for a major software developer, but branched out on my own two years ago. I have high standards for myself and others and wanted greater control over the creative and development process.
I just launched my first cell phone game to solid reviews and critical acclaim. Despite being very busy, I make it a point to find time to do the things I enjoy. And, since I spend the bulk of my day in front of computer screens, I spend my non working days hanging out with friends, hiking with my chocolate lab, Finneaus, or going to the movies. I'm looking for a like minded woman who has intelligence, a good sense of humor and good values.

From: Renee Greene – March 15, 2011 – 8:53 AM
To: Mark Finlay
Subject: Re: My Profile for Review

Say what?!? You haven't posted your profile yet. Dude! What have you been waiting for? I thought we were doing this together!

I've already been on three heinous online dates and endured a tongue lashing by one psycho cyber stalker and you haven't even gotten yourself out there? I am reviewing now....okay. Just read through. Only edits are hyphens added throughout – see attached. When you use compound adjectives to modify a noun, those adjectives need to be hyphenated. Sorry. But you asked for the "Grammar Hawk," no? Otherwise, looks great. Now post that bio!

From: Mark Finlay – March 15, 2011 – 9:03 AM
To: Renee Greene
Subject: Re: My Profile for Review

This is great. And I indeed asked for the "Grammar Hawk."

From: Renee Greene – March 15, 2011 – 10:26 AM
To: Shelley Manning
Subject: If you want anything done right, you have to do it yourself

Well, I've decided to take matters into my own hands. I spent a few hours last night scouring the Choose Jews site for my soul mate. And, I *think* I may just have found him. Here's an excerpt from his profile...

> After three years of toiling away on litigation suits representing big corporations and insurance companies – essentially helping them stick it to the little guy – I decided the deck was stacked too high in favor of big business. So, I recently quit my job and went to work for a non-profit legal aid. Every day, I get an immense satisfaction from helping good, decent people who have been screwed by the system.

> I never really thought online dating was for me. But after being out there in the dating scene for a while, I truly know now what I want and figured this was a way to find the quality person I'm searching for. I'm looking for a future partner to share my life and raise a family. My parents always said their job was to raise a productive, kind human being that makes the world a better place. Although they have both since passed away, I think they would be proud with how I've turned out. And, I want to honor them by doing the same with my children one day.

He sounds so wonderful. And, you can log on to see his profile. Very cute. I'm going to drop him an email shortly. Fingers crossed!

From: Shelley Manning – March 15, 2011 – 12:35 PM
To: Renee Greene
Subject: Re: If you want anything done right, you have to do it yourself

Wow. He does sound pretty great and I know how much you love that whole do-gooder thing. From now on, I will refer to him as Dudley Do Right. Two additional things in his favor: (1) He's easy on the eyes. VERY easy. (2) His parents aren't around. That means no Jewish mother in law.

From: Renee Greene – March 15, 2011 – 12:38 PM
To: Shelley Manning
Subject: Re: If you want anything done right, you have to do it yourself

Oh Shelley! You are so wicked!

From: Shelley Manning – March 15, 2011 – 12:42 PM
To: Renee Greene
Subject: Re: If you want anything done right, you have to do it yourself

I know, sweetie. That's why you keep me around. Good luck and let me know how it goes. Mwah! Mwah!

From: meet@choosejews.com/PRGal1981 – March 15, 2011 – 1:13 PM
To: meet@choosejews.com/LiveRight23
Subject: Hi

Hi Live Right 23. I was on the Choose Jews site and came across your profile. I must say I'm very impressed with your recent career change. How wonderful to feel so good about the work you are doing. I work in PR and sometimes feel like my time could be better spent helping to raise awareness for important issues and causes, instead of helping to sell toys and ovens.

Anyway, I think we might enjoy hanging out together. Why don't you check out my profile and let me know if you are interested in meeting up. Thanks.

From: Renee Greene – March 16, 2011 – 9:08 AM
To: Ashley Price; Shelley Manning
Subject: I need a stiff drink!

It's only 9:00 am and I already need a stiff drink. No sexual innuendo here, Shelley. I really just need a hard drink. Okay that probably didn't help matters much, huh? Let's just say I'm eager to meet at Flint's tonight after work. In? Out?

From: Shelley Manning – March 16, 2011 – 9:10 AM
To: Ashley Price; Renee Greene
Subject: Re: I need a stiff drink!

LMAO! In, in, in!

From: Ashley Price – March 16, 2011 – 9:15 AM
To: Shelley Manning; Renee Greene
Subject: Re: I need a stiff drink!

IN!!!! I will meet you at Flint's tonight with my new doo. Yes! I am taming the wild beast that is my hair with a new haircut and Brazilian blowout at Ra Jai salon (using that free $500 gift certificate from the casino party with Austin). So, be prepared to be wowed!

From: Shelley Manning – March 16, 2011 – 9:18 AM
To: Ashley Price; Renee Greene
Subject: Re: I need a stiff drink!

Brazilian Blowout? That sounds kinky.

From: Ashley Price – March 16, 2011 – 9:20 AM
To: Shelley Manning; Renee Greene
Subject: Re: I need a stiff drink!

It's nothing sexual, Shelley. It's a hair-straightening technique that takes out the frizz.

From: Shelley Manning – March 16, 2011 – 9:21 AM
To: Renee Greene
Subject: Fwd: Re: I need a stiff drink!

What's her problem? She's such a prude!

From: Ashley Price – March 16, 2011 – 9:21 AM
To: Renee Greene
Subject: Fwd: Re: I need a stiff drink!

What is her problem? She's such a whore!

From: Renee Greene – March 16, 2011 – 9:22 AM
To: Shelley Manning
Subject: Re: Fwd: Re: I need a stiff drink!

BEHAVE!

From: Renee Greene – March 16, 2011 – 9:22 AM
To: Ashley Price
Subject: Re: Fwd: Re: I need a stiff drink!

BEHAVE!

From: Renee Greene – March 16, 2011 – 9:23 AM
To: Shelley Manning; Ashley Price
Subject: Re: I need a stiff drink!

Okay. See you both tonight and looking forward to seeing the new you, Ashley. :)

From: Ashley Price – March 16, 2011 – 3:20 PM
To: Shelley Manning; Renee Greene
Subject: Re: I need a stiff drink!

Sorry ladies, but I won't be joining you tonight. My hair looks like…what's the word, oh yeah, poop. Ra Jai completely butchered it. I'm heading to a walk-in salon in the morning to see if they can fix it. I think I'm going to cry!

From: Renee Greene – March 16, 2011 – 3:35 PM
To: Shelley Manning; Ashley Price
Subject: Re: I need a stiff drink!

Oh Ashley. I'm so sorry. A bad haircut is just the worst. Remember that doozy I got in 9th grade? I wore a hat for 3 months until it grew out. Hopefully someone can salvage what's left. Hang in there.

From: Shelley Manning – March 16, 2011 – 3:45 PM
To: Renee Greene; Ashley Price
Subject: Re: I need a stiff drink!

I guess you get what you pay for, right?

From: Ashley Price – March 16, 2011 – 3:48 PM
To: Renee Greene; Shelley Manning
Subject: Re: I need a stiff drink!

Thanks Shelley. You sure know how to cheer a girl up. I'll talk with you guys later.

From: Shelley Manning – March 16, 2011 – 3:50 PM
To: Renee Greene
Subject: Re: I need a stiff drink!

OOPS! Guess she really doesn't get my humor. Oh well. See you tonight for a stiff one…and if we get lucky, a stiff one. Mwah! Mwah!

From: Renee Greene – March 18, 2011 – 9:02 AM
To: Mark Finlay
Subject: Front Line Scoop?

So? Any news from the front lines of the online dating wars?

From: Mark Finlay – March 18, 2011 – 10:12 AM
To: Renee Greene
Subject: Re: Front Line Scoop?

Oh, I haven't posted my profile just yet. I'm still looking for the right photo to post with it.

From: Renee Greene – March 18, 2011 – 10:18 AM
To: Shelley Manning
Subject: Fwd: Re: Front Line Scoop?

Can you believe this? Mark emailed last week and asked me to proof his online dating bio. And, he's still choosing a picture. He hasn't even gotten online yet.

From: Renee Greene – March 18, 2011 – 10:42 AM
To: Shelley Manning
Subject: Re: Fwd: Re: Front Line Scoop?

Send me his bio. I've got to see what he had to say about himself. "Anal, controlling, pain in the ass seeks a neat freak to share his coasters. Knowledge of cleaning products is a must ." HA! I do crack myself up. Gotta run. See you at Mel's tomorrow.

From: meet@choosejews.com/MusicMan22 – March 18, 2011 – 11:04 AM
To: meet@choosejews.com/PRGal1981
Subject: Spider Fire Fan

Hi there. I'm Matt. Loved your profile. I too am interested in the stylings of Spider Fire. In fact, I saw them a few weeks ago with some buddies in Santa Barbara. Listen, I was hoping you would check out my profile and perhaps write back. Have a great weekend.

From: meet@choosejews.com/PRGal1981 – March 18, 2011 – 11:22 AM
To: meet@choosejews.com/MusicMan22
Subject: Re: Spider Fire Fan

I was hoping to go, but it was sold out before I could get tickets. I heard it was rockin'. I did see them at The Greek last year, though. They were really great. Did you hear the rumors they may be breaking up? My friend said she heard that Gene's drug problem was getting really bad.

From: meet@choosejews.com/MusicMan22 – March 18, 2011 – 11:53 AM
To: meet@choosejews.com/PRGal1981
Subject: Re: Spider Fire Fan

Yeah, I heard that. But, he didn't seem real strung out when we saw them. With rumors, you just never know. Have you heard of Great Neck Weekly? They are a new band just coming on the scene. Kind of a combo of Spider Fire and Modern Joes? They are doing a small concert at the Wiltern next weekend. Would you want to go check it out on Friday night?

From: meet@choosejews.com/ PRGal1981 – March 18, 2011 – 11:59 AM
To: meet@choosejews.com/MusicMan22
Subject: Re: Spider Fire Fan

Sure. That would be great. Why don't I meet you there?

From: meet@choosejews.com/MusicMan22 – March 18, 2011 – 12:14 PM
To: meet@choosejews.com/PRGal1981
Subject: Re: Spider Fire Fan

That's cool. I have a sister and I know I wouldn't want some strange guy knowing where she lived. I'll meet you in front of will call at 7:30. Show starts at 8:00. See you then. My cell is 310/555-8275 and if you want to chat before then, give me a call.

From: Renee Greene – March 22, 2011 – 12:26 PM
To: Shelley Manning, Mark Finlay
Subject: The One!?!?!?

This could be it. His name is Matt Kaufman and he's a graphic designer for a surf company in Huntington Beach and loves my favorite bands. We've talked every night this week for HOURS. He's taking me to see Great Neck Weekly, which is a mix of Spider Fire and Modern Joes on Friday night. Keep your fingers crossed. This could be L-O-V-E. :)

From: Mark Finlay – March 22, 2011 – 1:30 PM
To: Shelley Manning; Renee Greene
Subject: Re: The One!?!?!?

Fingers crossed! Call me when you get home. Doesn't matter how late. I'll be up writing code. And, no, Shelley, "writing code" isn't code for something. It's just writing code.

From: Shelley Manning – March 22, 2011 – 3:07 PM
To: Renee Greene; Mark Finlay
Subject: Re: The One!?!?!?

Ha, Finlay! I *was* thinking it might be code for something.

Have fun, sweetie and call me when you're home.

From: Renee Greene – March 28, 2011 – 9:32 AM
To: Shelley Manning
Subject: Re: PER-FEC-TION!

Details, huh? Sounds like me writing to you instead of you writing to me. Normally I say that I have to live vicariously through you. But, for once in a long time, I really feel alive. So, here goes.

We met at the Wiltern about 7:30. He looked pretty much like his photo – absolutely adorable – but he seemed a bit taller than I had imagined. I think it's just the way he carries himself. True to photo, he was cute, but not overly gorgeous. His smile is a little crooked, but he has the most unbelievable, white teeth I've ever seen. I was so tempted to ask if they were real, but decided that I didn't want to spoil the illusion if they weren't. Anyway, his hair is a lighter sandy blond than in the photo and it made him kind of look like a professional volleyball player and part-time model for sun tan lotion.

We waited outside in line for about an hour before the show started and just talked. Just like on the phone, there were never any awkward silences. We had so much in common and he was just so interesting. He is a graphic designer and has shown his work at some small galleries at Bergamot Station. How cool is that? And, because he works in the marketing area, he actually understands what I do for a living. Kudos to him.

The concert was absolutely amazing. They are such a cool band. So much like Spider Fire but definitely with their own sound. I bought their CD at the event and am listening to it now as I'm writing to you instead of reviewing focus group research findings about cooking oil [YAWN!] I just can't seem to concentrate.

Anyway, after the concert ended, we walked across the street to a small coffee shop and had coffee. Well, he had coffee and I had a lemonade. He did sort of think it was strange that I'm 30 years old and I've never had a cup of coffee. But, he seemed to find it endearing. Extra points to him for that one.

Then, he walked me to my car and gave me the sweetest kiss goodnight. As I closed the door and he began to walk away, he turned around and knocked on my window. I rolled it down and – oh I'm just getting goose bumps thinking about it – he told me that he really had a great time and wanted to know when I was free for dinner. YEE HAW!

So, we have plans to go out on Wednesday. Hurrah! Do you have any idea how long it has been since I've been out on a second date?

From: Shelley Manning – March 28, 2011 – 11:46 AM
To: Renee Greene
Subject: Re: PER-FEC-TION!

Sweetie, that is so great! I'm thrilled for you. He sounds like a total gentleman…but I won't hold that against him. HA! I on the other hand, held myself all night against a really hot accountant (I know, that sounds like an oxymoron, but it's true) that I met at Flint's the other night. My only complaint. He was a tad bit too hairy…you know…down there. From this moment forward, he will be known as Ape.

From: MattKaufman782@easymailusa.com – March 28, 2011 – 12:03 PM
To: Renee Greene
Subject: Fun night

Hey Renee. I just wanted to drop you an email and tell you how much fun I had Saturday night. And, wanted you to have my real email address too. I never thought I could meet such a cool gal over the Internet. But, I'm lucky and happy to learn that I was wrong. Yes. You are reading this correctly. A man has admitted that indeed he was wrong. Anyway, hoping that you are having a great day at work and looking forward to dinner on Wednesday.

From: Renee Greene – March 28, 2011 – 12:08 PM
To: MattKaufman782@easymailusa.com
Subject: Re: Fun night

I was just about to email you to say thanks. That is so spooky. I had so much fun too. The concert was great but the company was even better. It is hard to believe I've met a Spider Fire fan that also has no problem admitting when he's wrong. What a rarity. Are you going to tell me that you actually have – shudder the thought – asked for directions? Or that you have put the toilet seat down? Hmm. What other male stereotypes can we bash here? <Ball is in your court>

From: MattKaufman782@easymailusa.com – March 28, 2011 – 12:16 PM
To: Renee Greene
Subject: Re: Fun night

Oh I see. We're going to play that game. Well, let me just imagine how many pairs of black shoes you have in your closet right now.

Wondering how I knew about that one, huh? As I mentioned, I do have a sister and she owns more pairs of black shoes than anyone I've ever met. <Ha! Just lobbed one back at you!>

About Wednesday, how about Korean BBQ? There's this great place I know and I would love to take you there.

From: Renee Greene – March 28, 2011 – 1:23 PM
To: MattKaufman782@easymailusa.com
Subject: Re: Fun night

Touché. I am the Queen of black shoes. In fact I have this theory that women own twelve pairs of black shoes – leather pumps, suede pumps, tall boots, short boots, flats, sandals, strappy sandals, lace-ups, etc. But, we only own one pair of athletic shoes. Men on the other hand own one pair of black shoes and twelve pairs of athletic shoes – tennis shoes, cleats, basketball shoes, deck shoes, cross trainers, running shoes, etc. You get the picture. To each his/her own vice, I say.

Korean BBQ sounds great. One of my buddies from college is Korean and his mom used to send him back to school after vacations with jars and jars filled with homemade kimchee. Dee-lish.

Well, I am off to the dentist for my annual cleaning. I'll talk with you later.

From: MattKaufman782@easymailusa.com – March 28, 2011 – 1:55 PM
To: Renee Greene
Subject: Re: Fun night

The dentist. Excellent. Love a woman with a sparkling clean mouth. Not that I don't love the occasional dirty talk. Oh, was that too much information? HA! HA!

Korean BBQ it is. Why don't I pick you up at your place? Is that okay or are you still worried I could be a murderer/serial killer?

From: Renee Greene – March 28, 2011 – 4:42 PM
To: MattKaufman782@easymailusa.com
Subject: Re: Fun night

Well, you could very well be a serial killer, but I'm willing to take the risk. I'll call you with my address. Looking forward to it.

From: Renee Greene – March 28, 2011 – 8:07 PM
To: Shelley Manning
Subject: Second Date!!!!!

A second date. Yes, you read correctly. I have a SECOND date. I don't even remember when was the last time I had a second date…with the same person. Matt is taking me to a little Korean BBQ place for dinner on Wednesday.

From: Shelley Manning – March 29, 2011 – 2:57 PM
To: Renee Greene
Subject: Re: Second Date!!!!!

Fab news! Crazy busy day. Gotta run. Cuddler just quit and we're having a cake for him. See you at Mel's tomorrow for lunch so we can talk further. Mwah! Mwah!

From: Shelley Manning – March 30, 2011 – 2:02 PM
To: Renee Greene
Subject: Cuddler Comments

Fun lunch as always. Gotta tell you, you had me in stitches. I've just never heard you so bruising before. Those jokes about the Cuddler – Ha-Larious! My favorite had to be his career change to weeper at a funeral home.

From: Renee Greene – March 30, 2011 – 2:12 PM
To: Shelley Manning
Subject: Re: Cuddler Comments

That was a good one, huh? I don't know what it is. I just can't help myself. It's fun to be a little mean sometimes.

From: Shelley Manning – March 30, 2011 – 2:15 PM
To: Renee Greene
Subject: Re: Cuddler Comments

Oh don't get me wrong. I love it when you are cruel and ruthless. It's just so not like you.

From: Renee Greene – March 30, 2011 – 2:17 PM
To: Shelley Manning
Subject: Re: Cuddler Comments

Well, get used to it baby. There's a new sheriff in town and her name is Supermodel Renee.

From: Shelley Manning – March 30, 2011 – 2:19 PM
To: Renee Greene
Subject: Re: Cuddler Comments

LOVE, LOVE, LOVE it.

From: Renee Greene – March 30 – 10:02 PM
To: Shelley Manning
Subject: Am I a joke?

Okay, I'm probably being TOTALLY paranoid. But, my SECOND DATE(!!!) with Matt is on April Fool's Day. After that fiasco with Valentine's Day, I'm thinking maybe he's just playing a trick on me.

From: Shelley Manning – March 31, 2011 – 8:42 AM
To: Renee Greene
Subject: Re: Am I a joke?

Being friends with you can be exhausting! Of course he's not playing a trick on you. He likes you. A woman with your impoverished levels of self-esteem just can't seem to see what the rest of us do. You're lovely, wonderful, funny, smart and all around great. How many times do I have to remind you – you are Supermodel Renee! So, go forth and enjoy! Mwah! Mwah!

From: Renee Greene – March 31, 2011 – 8:45 AM
To: Shelley Manning
Subject: Re: Am I a joke?

<blush!>

From: Renee Greene – April 2, 2011 – 11:15 AM
To: Shelley Manning
Subject: Candy Musings

Oh My God! So, Matt comes over last night with this big box of candy. Well, I didn't bother to read the card because we were leaving for dinner. So, I read the card when I get back and it says, "If this box of candy could only come close to embodying the sweetness of your smile, I would devour one every day." Good Lord!

From: Shelley Manning – April 4, 2011 – 8:42 AM
To: Renee Greene
Subject: Re: Candy Musings

Wow! Well, you do have a beautiful smile so the sentiment is true. But don't you think it is a little weird that he is being so effusive so early? Just be careful. I don't want you to get hurt. Sometimes guys say things because they want to get in good with you, or just with you, or just in you. The possibilities are really endless, aren't they? ;)

From: Renee Greene – April 4, 2011 – 9:56 AM
To: Shelley Manning
Subject: Re: Candy Musings

Oh Shelley. Just let me enjoy the attention for once.

From: Shelley Manning – April 4, 2011 – 10:02 AM
To: Renee Greene
Subject: Re: Candy Musings

You're right. You deserve it. I won't rain on your parade.

From: meet@choosejews.com/GoBucs428 – April 4, 2011 – 10:05 AM
To: meet@choosejews.com/PRGal1981
Subject: Hi!

Hi. I'm Ethan. I recently moved to LA from New York and am experiencing a bit of culture shock. It's a bit strange to not see anyone walking around.

I grew up in Columbus, Ohio (Go Bucs!) but went to college and grad school at NYU. I spent two years in the Peace Corps before returning to NY as a banking analyst. I know it sounds boring, but it's really not that bad. ;) I enjoy the outdoors, but also love to curl up on the couch with a good book or to watch a movie. Most important, I'm obsessed with peanut butter cups.

Anyway, you seem like a really fun and outgoing person and I think we have a lot in common. If you're interested, check out my profile and maybe we could talk.

From: meet@choosejews.com/PRGal1981 – April 4, 2011 – 10:17 AM
To: meet@choosejews.com/GoBucs428
Subject: Re: Hi!

Well, I have this theory that no one walks in LA but we all own treadmills. So even though the weather is nice all year round, we won't walk outside, but we'll walk in our houses. Strange creatures are we Los Angeleans. At any rate, I digress. I really appreciate your email. You sound like a great guy. But, I've recently met someone – through this site, so there's hope for us all ;) – and I'm kind of looking to see where that goes. But, good luck in meeting someone.

From: meet@choosejews.com/GoBucs428 – April 4, 2011 – 10:22 AM
To: meet@choosejews.com/PRGal1981
Subject: Re: Hi!

Strange Los Angeleans, indeed. Well, thank you for your nice note back. Good luck with this guy. I bet he's a lucky one.

From: Renee Greene – April 4, 2011 – 10:29 AM
To: member.services@choosejews.com
Subject: Profile on Hold

I am writing to request that you please hide my profile from viewing until further notice. My ID# is 49628; Screen Name: PRGal1981.

From: member.services@choosejews.com – April 4, 2011 – 10:32 AM
To: Renee Greene
Subject: Re: Profile on Hold

Profile has been hidden until further request.

From: Renee Greene – April 4, 2011 – 10:41 AM
To: Shelley Manning
Subject: On Hold

Just put my profile on hold. Got a nice email from a guy that was pretty cute and charming, and I felt so bad saying that I couldn't continue to talk with him because of Matt. Not that bad, though. I'm THRILLED to report that I'm dating a handsome, funny, smart, romantic and just plain wonderful man. Hurrah! I just wish I didn't have to go to NY tonight for a business trip. Three days in NY meeting with home decorating magazines for a client is usually my idea of a fun time. But, now that I have a man – yeah! – in my life. I just want to spend time with him.

From: Shelley Manning – April 4, 2011 – 11:08 AM
To: Renee Greene
Subject: Re: On Hold

That's a pretty big move, sweetie, giving up someone cute and charming when you've only known this guy for a week or so. Are you sure you want to count your chickens? What happened to not wanting things to move too fast – a la Valentine's Day desperado doctor?

From: Renee Greene – April 4, 2011 – 11:37 AM
To: Shelley Manning
Subject: Re: On Hold

Oh these chickens have been counted and are ready to hatch. He is WON-DER-FUL! I can't believe my luck meeting him. He loves my favorite band, is incredibly romantic and thoughtful, and thinks I'm funny. Yes! He laughs at my jokes. It is fast, but when it's right, it's right. Remember, you said you wouldn't rain on my parade.

From: Shelley Manning – April 4, 2011 – 1:15 PM
To: Renee Greene
Subject: Re: On Hold

Okay, okay. I'll keep my big mouth shut. I guess because I'm not a romantic at heart, I have a hard time believing in this whole "Love at First Sight" thing. But, I know you do and I do hope this works out. Good luck in NYC. Mwah! Mwah!

From: MattKaufman782@easymailusa.com – April 4, 2011 – 3:46 PM
To: Renee Greene
Subject: Safe Travels

Hi there. I know you are leaving tonight for your trip to New York. Just wanted to send a quick email wishing you a safe trip. I remember how you mentioned you hate to fly. Three days in NY with décor magazines. Sounds like a big snooze to me. But, if you were going to be there, I know it would be heavenly. If you have time, drop me an email or give me a call while you are there.

From: Renee Greene – April 4, 2011 – 4:12 PM
To: MattKaufman782@easymailusa.com
Subject: Re: Safe Travels

Thank you for your sweet message. I can see where a manly man like you would not want to be sitting around with a bunch of editors from home magazines. But actually, I'm really looking forward to it. It's usually pretty grueling to go from one interview to the next with a client, but it's fun to be in the editors' offices and get to see preview copies of the magazines. You know what a junkie I am for all of that stuff. Anyway, I'll drop you an email from the Big Apple.

From: MattKaufman782@easymailusa.com – April 5, 2011 – 4:26 PM
To: Renee Greene
Subject: Miss You!

I hope you got the flowers I sent to the hotel. I wasn't able to send a very long note with them, but wanted you to know that I give these flowers to you to show you how I miss the warmth of your heart and the entrancing beauty of your eyes. I wish I could be near you this week to feel the softness of your skin and the tenderness of your lips. My heart skips a beat every time I think about you. From all my heart, Matt.

From: Renee Greene – April 5, 2011 – 8:02 PM
To: Shelley Manning
Subject: Fwd: Miss You!

Holy cow. No one, not even during the three years I was with Derrick, has ever said such incredibly sweet, beautiful and romantic things to me. I feel like I'm going to melt.

From: Renee Greene – April 5, 2011 – 8:15 PM
To: MattKaufman782@easymailusa.com
Subject: Re: Miss You!

Thank you so much for the incredibly beautiful flowers and sweet email. I don't know how I got so lucky to meet such a romantic at heart. Looking forward to seeing you when I'm back. I'll call you when I get in.

From: Shelley Manning – April 5, 2011 – 9:22 PM
To: Renee Greene
Subject: Re: Fwd: Miss You!

JEEZ! This guy is really a ROMANTIC! I can't even believe this. The only time a guy has ever been this way with me was during a really awesome orgasm ;)

From: Renee Greene – April 5, 2011 – 9:32 PM
To: Shelley Manning
Subject: Re: Fwd: Miss You!

You are wicked, wicked, wicked. And, I love it.

From: Renee Greene – April 9, 2011 – 9:02 AM
To: Shelley Manning
Subject: This is IT!

Tonight is THE night. This is it! I don't know what makes me more excited. The fact that I'm going to sleep with Matt or that I'm going to end my year+ long affair with celibacy. It's been so long, I hope I remember what to do. Yes, yes, I know. It's like riding a bicycle. Let's just say that from what I remember, it was A LOT more fun than riding a bike.

We're having dinner at La Croquette (tres romantic) and then I'm going to ask him back up to my place. Hurrah! And, I got my legs and bikini waxed and am wearing sexy underwear. Nothing's gonna stop me now. I'm telling you, Shelley, this could be L-O-V-E.

From: Shelley Manning – April 9, 2011 – 10:16 AM
To: Renee Greene
Subject: Re: This is IT!

L-O-V-E or L-U-S-T? My goodness. I've known you since college and I've never known you to sound like such a tiger. Can't wait to hear all of the juicy details. Mwah! Mwah!

From: Renee Greene – April 10, 2011 – 3:03 AM
To: Shelley Manning
Subject: Wow! WOW! WOW!!!

Wow! I forgot how great sex could be. It had been entirely too long. He is PER-FECT. I'm telling you, this man is it. He has everything I've been looking for in a man. I need to buy Mark a gift to thank him for forcing me into this whole Internet dating thing and bringing this PER-FECT man into my life. God bless Mark.

From: Shelley Manning – April 10, 2011 – 12:26 PM
To: Renee Greene
Subject: Re: Wow! WOW! WOW!!!

God bless Finlay? Have you gone mad? I think a gift is a great idea. Perhaps a good lay…or a new set of coasters…or a pair of pliers to get the stick out of his ass…

From: Renee Greene – April 10, 2011 – 12:32 PM
To: Shelley Manning
Subject: Re: Wow! WOW! WOW!!!

Did I ever mention that you are wicked? I was thinking more along the lines of tickets to a concert or a game. I think he would enjoy something like that. I'll get on the web and figure it out.

From: Shelley Manning – April 10, 2011 – 12:41 PM
To: Renee Greene
Subject: Re: Wow! WOW! WOW!!!

Thank you for not reminding me that *I* hooked up with him.

From: Renee Greene – April 10, 2011 – 12:42 PM
To: Shelley Manning
Subject: Re: Wow! WOW! WOW!!!

I'd pretty much forgotten, until now since you reminded me. Thanks. Will do my best to keep that little factoid in my back pocket for future mocking.

From: Shelley Manning – April 10, 2011 – 12:44 PM
To: Renee Greene
Subject: Re: Wow! WOW! WOW!!!

Super! Wish *I* could forget. Sadly, although I have no memory of that incident, the scars are still forever with me.

From: Renee Greene – April 10, 2011 – 3:35 PM
To: Shelley Manning
Subject: Should I be worried?

Okay, it's been a day and Matt hasn't called. What do you think that means? Is that a bad sign?

From: Shelley Manning – April 10, 2011 – 5:26 PM
To: Renee Greene
Subject: Re: Should I be worried?

A day. Sweetie. Be realistic. Maybe he had to suddenly go out of town on business. Maybe he's working late. Maybe he isn't feeling well. It's only been a day. Way too early to start panicking.

From: Renee Greene – April 10, 2011 – 5:28 PM
To: Shelley Manning
Subject: Re: Should I be worried?

Maybe I'll call him.

From: Renee Greene – April 10, 2011 – 5:34 PM
To: Shelley Manning
Subject: Re: Should I be worried?

Okay, just left him a message and told him that I had such a great time the other night and I can't wait to see him again. Told him to call me.

From: Renee Greene – April 10, 2011 – 5:39 PM
To: Mark Finlay
Subject: Guy's Perspective

Hi Mark. Hope the project is going well. I know you are super busy writing code. And, maybe that's why you didn't answer the phone. But I need a guy's perspective on something. So, everything with Matt was going great. We talked on the phone ALL the time. He made these beautiful, sweeping romantic gestures and wrote/said the most beautiful things to me. And then, all of the sudden, he hasn't called or emailed at all. What could that mean?

From: Mark Finlay – April 11, 2011 – 1:13 AM
To: Renee Greene
Subject: Re: Guy's Perspective

Sorry. Just coming up for air. Major deadline looming. Give it another day or two. Maybe he's just busy with work like me.

From: Renee Greene – April 11, 2011 – 8:02 AM
To: Mark Finlay
Subject: Re: Guy's Perspective

Thanks. I was starting to panic a bit. But, you're right. He might be under a major deadline or something. Good luck meeting your deadline.

From: Renee Greene – April 13, 2011 – 9:02 AM
To: Shelley Manning
Subject: Re: Should I be worried?

Okay, it's been three days and he hasn't returned my call. Maybe there is something wrong with his machine. I'll email.

From: Renee Greene – April 13, 2011 – 9:07 AM
To: MattKaufman782@easymailusa.com
Subject: A little worried

Hi Matt. Hope you are okay. It's been a few days since we talked and I was getting a little worried. I also left a message for you on your answering machine. Figure you just didn't get it. Anyway, give me a call because I'm excited for us to go out again.

From: MattKaufman782@easymailusa.com – April 13, 2011 – 12:36 PM
To: Renee Greene
Subject: Re: A little worried

Hey Renee. Yeah, I got your message. I've just been really busy. You know, I think you're a great gal. But, I'm just really not ready for a relationship. I'm really looking to focus my energies on work. Maybe in a few months things will be different and I'll be able to be involved. But, for right now, I think this just isn't going to work.

From: Renee Greene – April 13, 2011 – 12:53 PM
To: Shelley Manning; Mark Finlay
Subject: Fwd: Re: A little worried

Bastard! Why did I think dating in the online world would be any different than dating in the regular world. Men suck. I feel like such an idiot.

What is wrong with me? Why doesn't anyone want to be with me? I know I've only known him for a few weeks and it seems like Derrick and I were together forever, but it hurts just as badly. And don't give me that bullshit about it making me stronger and that we learn something from every relationship. What I've learned is that a charming, handsome and smart man slept with me and then decided he didn't want to go out with me anymore. I don't know how that is supposed to make me anything but depressed.

I just don't understand. Why would he spend weeks telling me how much he liked me and how much fun he was having? Okay, well, it's obvious now. He was just trying to get me in the sack. So, that begs the question…do I just absolutely suck in bed or is he just a serial dumper?

And why was I such a sucker? Why did I fall for all his smooth lines and obvious false romanticism?

I'm sitting in my office – thank goodness I'm not in an open cubicle – and I can't stop crying. I think I'm going home to take a sick day.

From: Shelley Manning – April 13, 2011 – 1:15 PM
To: Renee Greene; Mark Finlay
Subject: Re: Fwd: Re: A little worried

Oh sweetie. I'm so sorry. He is truly the scum of the earth. You should call that prick and tell him exactly what you think of him. Better yet, I'll call him and tell him what an asshole he is.

From: Renee Greene – April 13, 2011 – 1:22 PM
To: Shelley Manning; Mark Finlay
Subject: Re: Fwd: Re: A little worried

Thank you for not saying I told you so. I know you were trying to tell me not to get my hopes up and I wasn't listening. I should have.

From: Shelley Manning – April 13, 2011 – 1:31 PM
To: Renee Greene; Mark Finlay
Subject: Re: Fwd: Re: A little worried

I'm not worried about being right. I'm worried about you. So, are you going to call him?

From: Renee Greene – April 13, 2011 – 1:33 PM
To: Shelley Manning; Mark Finlay
Subject: Re: Fwd: Re: A little worried

I don't think I could stand to hear his voice. I just can't believe this. I just can't.

From: Shelley Manning – April 13, 2011 – 1:36 PM
To: Renee Greene; Mark Finlay
Subject: Re: Fwd: Re: A little worried

Well, you're going to say *something*. At least send him a scathing email to tell him how horrid he has been.

From: Mark Finlay – April 13, 2011 – 2:25 PM
To: Renee Greene; Shelley Manning
Subject: Re: Fwd: Re: A little worried

Oh Renee. I'm so sorry. The guy sounds like a total jerk. You deserve so much better. But, we're not all like this ass or Derrick. There are good guys out there.

From: Renee Greene – April 13, 2011 – 11:56 PM
To: Shelley Manning; Mark Finlay
Subject: Rough Draft

Matt: I didn't think I would have the nerve to say this to your face or on the phone. Luckily we started this whole thing on email and you cowardly tried to end it that way too. So, I think it's fitting my final reply to you comes via email as well.

I don't understand why you spent weeks romancing me only to sleep with me and abruptly end things. I don't understand how you say things like "The sun should always shine on you so that your smile will last forever" and then overnight decide that work is more important than a relationship.

I deserve better. I deserve someone who is truthful with their feelings and honest in communicating their emotions. At the same time, I deserve someone who holds back on their feelings until it is appropriate to express them, so that they aren't leading me on. I also deserve what I thought you were...someone who is charming, smart, romantic, caring, thoughtful and honest.

From: Shelley Manning – April 14, 2011 – 8:53 AM
To: Renee Greene; Mark Finlay
Subject: Re: Rough Draft

All I can say is GOOD FOR YOU. I can tell you put a lot of thought, emotion and your fair share of tears into this. Hopefully you feel a bit better. I'm so impressed and think you should send it right away. Would LOVE to know if you get a response.

From: Mark Finlay – April 14, 2011 – 9:16 AM
To: Renee Greene; Shelley Manning
Subject: Re: Rough Draft

Wow! I would not want to be on the receiving end of that message. Well done, Renee. Well done.

From: Renee Greene – April 14, 2011 – 10:02 AM
To: Shelley Manning; Mark Finlay
Subject: Re: Rough Draft

I do feel a little better. I think it is really cathartic to be able to put pen to paper – or in this case, fingers to keyboard – and really be able to articulate what you're feeling.

I think if I had to do this in person, or over the phone, I'd be more of a wreck than I was writing and rewriting this until it was perfect.

From: Shelley Manning – April 14, 2011 – 10:07 AM
To: Renee Greene; Mark Finlay
Subject: Re: Rough Draft

Well, I think it's fantastic. Heart felt, yet dignified. He deserves far worse. But, knowing you, you don't want to be too cruel.

From: Renee Greene – April 14, 2011 – 10:12 AM
To: Shelley Manning; Mark Finlay
Subject: Re: Rough Draft

Thanks. I didn't want to have this come across as the rantings of someone dumped. I wanted him to realize that his actions were cruel and unfair.

From: Shelley Manning – April 14, 2011 – 10:23 AM
To: Renee Greene; Mark Finlay
Subject: Re: Rough Draft

Well, I think you did just that. Again, would LOVE to know if he emails you back or calls. Keep me posted. And put that profile back online. A man who really *is* all of those things is out there waiting for you. Speaking of which, whatever happened to Dudley Do Right?

From: Renee Greene – April 14, 2011 – 10:25 AM
To: Shelley Manning
Subject: Re: Rough Draft

He never emailed me back.

From: Shelley Manning – April 14, 2011 – 10:27 AM
To: Renee Greene
Subject: Re: Rough Draft

Oooh, ouch! So sorry, sweetie. Well, certainly his loss. You are clearly too good for him too.

From: Renee Greene – April 14, 2011 – 10:32 AM
To: Shelley Manning
Subject: Re: Rough Draft

Do you really believe that stuff? Clearly if I was too good for these guys, *I'd* be the one giving them the brush off.

From: Shelley Manning – April 14, 2011 – 10:34 AM
To: Renee Greene
Subject: Re: Rough Draft

Well, I think you're too good for *me*. Feel better?

From: Renee Greene – April 14, 2011 – 10:36 AM
To: Shelley Manning
Subject: Re: Rough Draft

A little. ;) Thanks!

From: Mark Finlay – April 14, 2011 – 12:02 PM
To: Renee Greene; Shelley Manning
Subject: Re: Rough Draft

Don't fall over, but I agree 100% with Shelley.

From: Renee Greene – April 14, 2011 – 12:07 PM
To: Shelley Manning; Mark Finlay
Subject: Re: Rough Draft

That was just the laugh I needed. Thanks guys. You're the best. Okay, back online (RELUCTANTLY), I go. But, I'm in a fragile state. I think cocktails at Flint's may make me feel better. I'll call you later to make plans. Love you!

From: Renee Greene – April 14, 2011 – 12:16 PM
To: MattKaufman782@easymailusa.com
Subject: The Way it SHOULD Be

Matt: I didn't think I would have the nerve to say this to your face or on the phone. Luckily we started this whole thing on email and you cowardly tried to end it that way too. So, I think it's fitting my final reply to you comes via email as well.

I don't understand why you spent weeks romancing me only to sleep with me and abruptly end things. I don't understand how you say things like "The sun should always shine on you so that your smile will last forever" and then overnight decide that work is more important than a relationship.

I deserve better. I deserve someone who is truthful with their feelings and honest in communicating their emotions. At the same time, I deserve someone who holds back on their feelings until it is appropriate to express them, so that they aren't leading me on. I also deserve what I thought you were…someone who is charming, smart, romantic, caring, thoughtful and honest.

From: Renee Greene – April 14, 2011 – 12:18 PM
To: member.services@choosejews.com
Subject: My Profile

I am writing to request that you please place my profile back online. My ID# is 49628; Screen Name: PRGal1981.

From: member.services@choosejews.com – April 14, 2011 – 12:20 PM
To: Renee Greene
Subject: Re: My Profile

Profile has been reinstated.

CHAPTER FIVE – DATING PURGATORY

From: Renee Greene– April 17, 2011 – 2:30 AM
To: Shelley Manning
Subject: One more try

Couldn't sleep, so I logged onto Choose Jews and was scrolling through the eligible bachelors last night and came across another interesting profile. He seems really cool. I pasted an excerpt below. I drive a hybrid and always use an aluminum water bottle. So, I'm going to give it one more proactive try. I'll keep you posted.

> So, you might be wondering why I picked the screen name EarthMan. No, I'm not an alien trying to blend in with you humans. Wouldn't that be something?! No, I work for the Parks Service on public education campaigns about recycling and composting. I'm pretty passionate about the importance of protecting the earth and have tried to integrate some of the best practices I've learned on the job into my daily life. I'm hoping to find someone with a similar dedication.

From: meet@choosejews.com/PRGal1981 – April 17 – 9:33 AM
To: meet@choosejews.com/EarthMan2011
Subject: Hi

Hi there EarthMan. I saw your profile and thought you seemed like a really interesting, smart and fun person. I was hoping you would check out my profile and then perhaps we can meet. I'll bring my hybrid! ;)

From: Shelley Manning– April 17 – 10:18 AM
To: Renee Greene
Subject: Re: One more try

Please tell me you didn't email him right after emailing me. No offense, sweetie, but nothing smacks more of desperation than getting an email from a girl at 2:30 am.

From: Renee Greene – April 17, 2011 – 11:32 AM
To: Shelley Manning
Subject: Re: One more try

No. I didn't email him at 2:30 am. Who am I, Tiffany? No, I waited until 9:33 am to be exact.

From: Shelley Manning – April 17, 2011 – 11:56 AM
To: Renee Greene
Subject: Re: One more try

Good girl. Yes, he seems very cool and cute. I will send good positive vibes your way for this one. Mwah! Mwah!

From: meet@choosejews.com/EarthMan2011 – April 18, 2011 – 4:42 PM
To: meet@choosejews.com/PRGal1981
Subject: Re: Hi

You drive a hybrid? Then I'm in. Seriously, I read your profile and love your sense of humor. Let's meet. Do you know the "O" in Venice? Maybe we could try for brunch on Sunday around 11? Oh, and my real name is Danny.

From: meet@choosejews.com/PRGal1981 – April 18, 2011 – 6:02 PM
To: meet@choosejews.com/EarthMan2011
Subject: Re: Hi

Hi Danny. I'm Renee. I'm not familiar with the "O" but love trying new places. I'll meet you there on Sunday at 11:00. Have a good week.

From: meet@choosejews.com/ChefChad – April 19, 2011 – 11:18 AM
To: meet@choosejews.com/PRGal1981
Subject:

Looked @ ur profile & u seem like a gr8 MOT. I M A chef so like 2 cook What's ur #?

From: meet@choosejews.com/ PRGal1981 – April 19, 2011 – 1:45 PM
To: meet@choosejews.com/ChefChad
Subject: Re:

Hi there. It's not too often I meet a guy who likes to cook as much as I do, but I guess when you are a chef there's a big incentive (read: paycheck) to spend time in the kitchen. Where do you work? Where did you train? What do you focus on?

From: meet@choosejews.com/ChefChad – April 19, 2011 – 2:02 PM
To: meet@choosejews.com/PRGal1981
Subject: Re:

LOL! M4C? I'll share my kitchen secrets w/ u. *$ Sat?

From: meet@choosejews.com/ PRGal1981 – April 19, 2011 – 3:12 PM
To: meet@choosejews.com/ChefChad
Subject: Re:

Kitchen secrets? I'm sold! What does Saturday late morning look like for you? Would you want to meet around 10:00 at the Coffee Shack in Brentwood?

From: meet@choosejews.com/ChefChad – April 19, 2011 – 4:18 PM
To: meet@choosejews.com/PRGal1981
Subject: Re:

Work till 2, 11?

From: meet@choosejews.com/ PRGal1981 – April 19, 2011 – 5:02 PM
To: meet@choosejews.com/ChefChad
Subject: Re:

Of course. I forgot that Friday is probably a super busy night. I imagine the social life of a chef must be rough with all of the late night hours and working weekend. 11:00 is great. See you then.

From: meet@choosejews.com/ChefChad – April 19, 2011 – 5:05 PM
To: meet@choosejews.com/PRGal1981
Subject: Re:

TTYL

From: Renee Greene – April 19, 2011 – 5:15 PM
To: Shelley Manning; Mark Finlay
Subject: Kitchen Secrets

Hi guys. Well, I'm back online and have met a chef who wants to share his kitchen secrets with me and a guy who works for the parks department. We're meeting Saturday at 11:00 at Coffee Shack/Sunday at a restaurant in West Hollywood respectively. I'll call you both when I get home.

From: Shelley Manning – April 19, 2011 – 6:22 PM
To: Renee Greene; Mark Finlay
Subject: Re: Kitchen Secrets

Kitchen secrets? Is that code for something sexual I'm unaware of? Hope so for your sake. Have fun!

From: Mark Finlay – April 19, 2011 – 9:26 PM
To: Renee Greene; Shelley Manning
Subject: Re: Kitchen Secrets

A chef? Perfect for you. Happy to be the recipient of these new kitchen secrets, as long as it's not code for something sexual. LOL! No offense or anything. It's just that you're like a sister to me.

From: meet@choosejews.com/FunDays222 – April 20, 2011 – 8:03 PM
To: meet@choosejews.com/PRGal1981
Subject: No such thing as bad PR?

Hi PR Gal. I take it you work in PR, no? I know what you're thinking. This guy is so intuitive. Yes, it's true. I pride myself on seeing between the lines. ;) I liked your profile, so check mine out and let me know if you want to chat?

From: meet@choosejews.com/ PRGal1981 – April 21, 2011 – 9:56 AM
To: meet@choosejews.com/FunDays222
Subject: Re: No such thing as bad PR?

Hi Barry. Thanks for your email. I must say, you certainly did figure me out right away. You must be really smart. ;) So, here are a few other things for you to think about…

- Who is your favorite Brady?
- If Bionic Woman and Wonder Woman got in a fight, who would win?
- What is the last book you read or are currently reading?
- Aside from what's in your profile, what else do you like to do?

Looking forward to hearing back from you.

From: meet@choosejews.com/FunDays222 – April 21, 2011 – 11:16 AM
To: meet@choosejews.com/PRGal1981
Subject: Re: No such thing as bad PR?

Well, PR Gal. I certainly like the way you think. Your questions are awesome. Here are some answers…

My favorite Brady is Jan. I'm the middle child with an older sister and brother and two younger sisters. Yes, five kids. My parents certainly were busy. Sadly, my older sister and one of my younger sisters live in DC and Chicago so we don't see each other that often. But, my brother and other younger sister are local, so we hang out a lot.

Not just a girl fight, but a super girl fight. Love it! This is a hard one. I've watched my share of MMA (mixed martial arts, for the uninitiated) and I gotta say, this would be too close to call. I'm not much of a gambler, so I wouldn't feel comfortable placing a bet on either of these ladies against the other.

Currently reading? Sad to say that I don't have much time to read. Between work, working out and just taking care of daily life, reading seems to have fallen by the wayside. Hope that doesn't knock me out of contention for a date with you.

Other interests, huh? Well, to be perfectly frank, I like to have sex…a lot. Hope to hear back from you.

From: Renee Greene – April 21, 2011 – 12:17 PM
To: Shelley Manning
Subject: Fwd: Re: No such thing as bad PR?

Oh my! Not sure what to make of this. Does this mean he likes to have a lot of sex or likes to have sex often? How am I supposed to respond?

From: Shelley Manning – April 21, 2011 – 12:19 PM
To: Renee Greene
Subject: Re: Fwd: Re: No such thing as bad PR?

Ask him! Would love to see his response?

From: Renee Greene – April 21, 2011 – 12:31 PM
To: Shelley Manning
Subject: Re: Fwd: Re: No such thing as bad PR?

So what do you think of this…

Well, that certainly is a lot to share. So, um, about that last point. Does that mean you like to have a lot of sex, or you like to have sex often?

From: Shelley Manning – April 21, 2011 – 12:33 PM
To: Renee Greene
Subject: Re: Fwd: Re: No such thing as bad PR?

Got for it. It's all anonymous, right?

From: meet@choosejews.com/PRGal1981 – April 21, 2011 – 12:41 PM
To: meet@choosejews.com/FunDays222
Bcc: Shelley Manning
Subject: Re: No such thing as bad PR?

Well, that certainly is a lot to share. So, um, about that last point. Does that mean you like to have a lot of sex, or you like to have sex often?

From: meet@choosejews.com/FunDays222 – April 21, 2011 – 3:09 PM
To: meet@choosejews.com/PRGal1981
Bcc: Shelley Manning
Subject: Re: No such thing as bad PR?

I like to have a lot of sex…often. So, wanna have a drink?

From: Renee Greene – April 21, 2011 – 3:14 PM
To: Shelley Manning
Subject: Fwd: Re: No such thing as bad PR?

Ew! See below. Should I just ignore it?

From: Shelley Manning – April 21, 2011 – 3:26 PM
To: Renee Greene
Subject: Re: Fwd: Re: No such thing as bad PR?

I got bcc'd on his response. Hilarious! I think you should go out with him. He sounds fun.

From: Renee Greene – April 21, 2011 – 3:28 PM
To: Shelley Manning
Subject: Re: Fwd: Re: No such thing as bad PR?

Maybe I should just give him your number. ;) From cuddler to nymphomaniac, right?

From: meet@choosejews.com/ChefChad – April 22, 2011 – 4:30 PM
To: meet@choosejews.com/PRGal1981
Subject: CYT

From: Renee Greene – April 22, 2011 – 4:39 PM
To: Shelley Manning
Subject: Fwd: CYT

Huh? What does CYT mean?

From: Shelley Manning – April 22, 2011 – 4:41 PM
To: Renee Greene
Subject: Re: Fwd: CYT

No clue. Let me know when you figure it out. Mwah! Mwah!

From: Renee Greene – April 22, 2011 – 5:56 PM
To: Shelley Manning
Subject: Re: Fwd: CYT

"See you tomorrow." Who knew?

From: Shelley Manning – April 22, 2011 – 6:25 PM
To: Renee Greene
Subject: Re: Fwd: CYT

Have fun and call me or email when you're back. I've got another date with a guy who we shall refer to as the Human Vacuum. He sort of sucks your tongue in when he's kissing you. I'm not a fan of the technique, but I'm willing to see what other techniques he's got lurking in that beautiful bod of his. TTYL as your date tomorrow would say. ;)

From: Renee Greene – April 23, 2011 – 2:28 PM
To: Shelley Manning
Subject: Not Gr8!

Ugh! Chad is a serial texter. I need a frickin' translator to decipher his emails.
He must have gotten and responded to a dozen - and though I'm prone to exaggeration when it comes to complaining about my dismal love life, I'm likely <u>underestimating</u> here – a dozen texts during our date. He even snapped a picture of me and posted it on his Facebook page right then and there.

From: Shelley Manning – April 23, 2011 – 11:32 PM
To: Renee Greene
Subject: Re: Not Gr8!

R u kidding? Ha! (Sorry, couldn't resist.) That is so annoying. And rude, I must say.

Sorry I wasn't home when you called. I was with a gentleman who I shall refer to as the Equestrian. Quite a ride!

From: Renee Greene – April 23, 2011 – 11:58 PM
To: Shelley Manning
Subject: Re: Not Gr8!

Amen, sister. Both annoying and rude. And of course he texted me an hour later for another date. Told him "2BZ but 10Q." Translation: "Too busy, but thank you" for us normal people. Gotta get to bed. Have my date tomorrow with EarthMan. I'll send you and Mark the details in the morning.

From: Shelley Manning – April 24, 2011 – 12:01 AM
To: Renee Greene
Subject: Re: Not Gr8!

LMAO!

From: Renee Greene – April 24, 2011 – 9:43 AM
To: Shelley Manning; Mark Finlay
Subject: The "O"

Not the "Big O," Shelley. Although I figured the subject line would get your attention. No, I'm going to a restaurant this morning called the "O" with EarthMan. His real name is Danny something or other. But, it's a public place and as usual, I will call or email when I get home.

From: Shelley Manning – April 24, 2011 – 10:32 AM
To: Renee Greene; Mark Finlay
Subject: Re: The "O"

Yes, you certainly know how to grab a girl's attention, don't you? Well, have fun sweetie. And, maybe if you get lucky, the "O" will result in the "Big O" after all.

From: Renee Greene – April 24, 2011 – 10:34 AM
To: Shelley Manning; Mark Finlay
Subject: Re: The "O"

"O" no you didn't!

From: Mark Finlay – April 24, 2011 – 11:22 AM
To: Renee Greene; Shelley Manning
Subject: Re: The "O"

Should I really be getting cc'd on these emails? I feel like a voyeur! Have fun and be safe.

From: Shelley Manning – April 24, 2011 – 11:24 AM
To: Renee Greene; Mark Finlay
Subject: Re: The "O"

Oh – or should I say "O" – didn't see you there, Finlay. Sorry. I'll be more careful next time.

From: Renee Greene – April 24, 2011 – 1:58 PM
To: Shelley Manning; Mark Finlay
Subject: O is for Organic

Well, I figured out that the "O" in "O" stands for…you guessed it…organic. It was an all-organic restaurant. And, I gotta say, the food was pretty good. Wish I could say the same for Danny. It started out just fine. He is really cute and – at first – quite charming. But, as brunch wore on, he and his "earthy" ways started to wear on my nerves. BIG TIME!

Did you know that 20,000 deaths occur every year in developing countries from pesticide poisoning by growing conventional cotton? Or that the livestock industry is one of the largest contributors to environmental degradation worldwide? Or that ground water can be improved through organic farming methods? Neither did it. But I do now.

I drive a hybrid. I take my own grocery bags to the store. I even recycle my batteries. Can you two say that? But, you would have thought I was the single biggest contributor to the downfall of the entire ecosystem. I don't eat the right foods, shop the right stores or wear the right clothes.

The date ended with a mutual, but still "O" so awkward acknowledgment that this was not a love match. I'm going to drown my sorrows with a juicy steak and highly-processed can of frosting.

From: Shelley Manning – April 24, 2011 – 2:30 PM
To: Renee Greene; Mark Finlay
Subject: Re: O is for Organic

"O" no! Put down the frosting. Step away from the frosting. Seriously, don't get discouraged. Get off the couch (because I know that's where you are!), open up a window to let in some fresh air and remember how great you are, sweetie.

From: Mark Finlay – April 24, 2011 – 6:57 PM
To: Renee Greene; Shelley Manning
Subject: Re: O is for Organic

I ech"O" what Shelley just said. Hard to believe, I know. But really, you're the best, Renee. It'll happen for you. I just know it.

From: Renee Greene – April 24, 2011 – 7:28 PM
To: Shelley Manning; Mark Finlay
Subject: Re: O is for Organic

Thanks guys. I'm so lucky to have friends like you two.

From: meet@choosejews.com/FunDays222 – April 28, 2011 – 1:08 PM
To: meet@choosejews.com/PRGal1981
Bcc: Shelley Manning
Subject: Re: No such thing as bad PR?

Haven't heard back from you? Is this because I don't read?

From: Shelley Manning – April 28, 2011 – 1:17 PM
To: Renee Greene
Subject: Fwd: Re: No such thing as bad PR?

OMG! I needed a good laugh. You should email him back and say that nymphomaniacs are fine, but illiterates are not.

From: Renee Greene – April 28, 2011 – 1:19 PM
To: Shelley Manning
Subject: Re: Fwd: Re: No such thing as bad PR?

Yikes!

From: Renee Greene – May 3, 2011 – 2:36 PM
To: Shelley Manning; Ashley Price
Subject: One for the books

Well, ladies. Per my subject line, this truly is one for the books. I know you two, of all people, will totally appreciate this story. So, I'm sitting at Tom's Bistro with a colleague from work and a client having a lunch meeting. About half way through, the waitress walks over and hands me a note and says it's from a gentleman in the restaurant. (I still don't know who he was.)

I open it up and it says, "I'm on a REALLY BAD first date right now. Not only are we not clicking, but I'm completely distracted looking at you across the room. I hope you won't be totally offended by this, but I would really like to take you out on a date. Obviously, I can't come over there and talk with you now. So, here is my contact info. I hope you'll email or call me. P.S. I NEVER do this."

And…go!

From: Shelley Manning – May 3, 2011 – 4:42 PM
To: Ashley Price; Renee Greene
Subject: Re: One for the books

Sounds like a VERY smart guy to have noticed you from across the room and sensed how awesome you are. Call him. What have you got to lose?

From: Ashley Price – May 3, 2011 – 6:07 PM
To: Shelley Manning; Renee Greene
Subject: Re: One for the books

What have you got to lose? Your dignity! I say this guy sounds like a total jerk. What's to say that he won't be scouting around for something better while *you're* on a first date with him?

From: Shelley Manning – May 4, 2011 – 8:29 AM
To: Ashley Price; Renee Greene
Subject: Re: One for the books

Of course you would have to be so pessimistic about this. I'm sure you've been on a date that isn't going well. So, why punish him just because he happened to see Renee at that moment, as opposed to a time when he was with some buddies, walking his dog, going to the drycleaners, etc.?

From: Ashley Price – May 4, 2011 – 10:02 AM
To: Shelley Manning; Renee Greene
Subject: Re: One for the books

Why are you so sure I've been on a bad date? Are you implying that I'm a bad date? Regardless, he didn't see her with some friends, walking his dog or going to the drycleaners.

From: Shelley Manning – May 4, 2011 – 11:17 AM
To: Ashley Price; Renee Greene
Subject: Re: One for the books

Of course I wouldn't be implying that. I just mean that we all go on dates that don't end up the way we planned. Don't hold it against the guy. Give it a try, Renee.

From: Shelley Manning – May 4, 2011 – 11:18 AM
To: Renee Greene
Subject: Yes, I am!

Of course I'm implying she's a bad date.

From: Renee Greene – May 4, 2011 – 11:20 AM
To: Shelley Manning
Subject: Re: Yes, I am!

Behave!

From: Shelley Manning – May 4, 2011 – 11:22 AM
To: Renee Greene
Subject: Re: Yes, I am!

But, didn't think she'd call me out on it. I actually give her props for that.

From: Renee Greene – May 4, 2011 – 11:25 AM
To: Shelley Manning
Subject: Re: Yes, I am!

Are you starting to <gulp!> like Ashley?

From: Shelley Manning – May 4, 2011 – 11:29 AM
To: Renee Greene
Subject: Re: Yes, I am!

Don't get ahead of yourself, sweetie. I just respect the feistiness. Wish some of that backbone would transfer to you, my darling friend.

From: Renee Greene – May 4, 2011 – 11:31 AM
To: Shelley Manning
Subject: Re: Yes, I am!

Me too.

From: Ashley Price – May 4, 2011 – 1:42 PM
To: Shelley Manning; Renee Greene
Subject: Re: One for the books

He's a total stranger. Why would she go out with a total stranger?

From: Shelley Manning – May 4, 2011 – 1:51 PM
To: Ashley Price; Renee Greene
Subject: Re: One for the books

So, she doesn't know him. Big deal. It's no different than the online dating she's been doing.

From: Ashley Price – May 4, 2011 – 1:52 PM
To: Shelley Manning; Renee Greene
Subject: Re: One for the books

Online dating? Renee, you've been using an online dating service? Since when? Why didn't you tell me?

From: Shelley Manning – May 4, 2011 – 1:53 PM
To: Renee Greene
Subject: SO, SO, SO, SO, SO SORRY!!!

UGH! I'm sooooooooooooo sorry. I completely forgot that the online dating scene was a secret from her. I'm soooooooooooo sorry. Please, don't hate me.

From: Renee Greene – May 4, 2011 – 1:54 PM
To: Shelley Manning
Subject: Re: SO, SO, SO, SO, SO SORRY!!!

CRAP! Don't worry. I know you just got caught up in trying to win the argument. I was really hoping to keep this from her until I got married – or at least engaged. But, she was going to find out sometime. I'll just get it over with now.

From: Renee Greene – May 4, 2011 – 2:37 PM
To: Shelley Manning; Ashley Price
Subject: Re: One for the books

Oh, it's really not that big of a deal. I'm trying the whole online dating thing with Mark – well not dating Mark, but you know what I mean. It's only been for a few months and I've only gone out on a handful of dates and none of them have been very eventful. I didn't mention it because I didn't want to get anyone's hopes up that anything would come of it.

From: Shelley Manning – May 4, 2011 – 2:39 PM
To: Renee Greene
Subject: Bravo!

Nice spin. You really are in PR.

From: Renee Greene – May 4, 2011 – 2:41 PM
To: Shelley Manning
Subject: Re: Bravo!

It's a gift. ;)

From: Ashley Price – May 4, 2011 – 3:17 PM
To: Shelley Manning; Renee Greene
Subject: Re: One for the books

Well, I'm not surprised it hasn't panned out. I can't imagine the kind of men who are online. But good luck anyway. And keep me posted.

From: Renee Greene – May 4, 2011 – 5:02 PM
To: Shelley Manning; Ashley Price
Subject: Re: One for the books

Will do. Anyway, I agree with Ashley. While I do commend this guy for his honesty – he could have just lied and said he saw me across the room – I think it's a rather uncool move to hit on me when he's on a date with someone else. So, I will disregard. But, off to grab a blended to celebrate both my undeniable hotness and moral superiority. ;)

From: Mark Finlay – May 8, 2011 – 9:02 PM
To: Renee Greene
Subject: It's Official

Okay, I'm officially online. Will keep you posted.

From: Mark Finlay – May 10, 2011 – 10:09 AM
To: Renee Greene
Subject: Busy Tonight?

What are you doing tonight? Can we meet for a coffee (or in your case a blended)?

From: Renee Greene – May 10, 2011 – 10:15 AM
To: Mark Finlay
Subject: Re: Busy Tonight?

I'm free tonight. What did you have in mind?

From: Mark Finlay – May 10, 2011 – 10:20 AM
To: Renee Greene
Subject: Re: Busy Tonight?

I'm overwhelmed. Not emotionally with flattery, but physically overwhelmed. I got 16 emails between last night and this morning after posting my bio.

From: Renee Greene – May 10, 2011 – 10:22 AM
To: Mark Finlay
Subject: Re: Busy Tonight?

16! That's got to be some kind of record, wouldn't you say?

From: Mark Finlay – May 10, 2011 – 10:25 AM
To: Renee Greene
Subject: Re: Busy Tonight?

I've printed out all of their emails, bios and photos and sorted them into piles of yes, no and maybe. Hoping I can review with you.

From: Renee Greene – May 10, 2011 – 10:27 AM
To: Mark Finlay
Subject: Re: Busy Tonight?

You got it. I'll meet you at 8:00. This should be fun.

From: Renee Greene – May 10, 2011 – 10:33 AM
To: Shelley Manning
Subject: Certifiable, no?

So, Mark *FINALLY* got his bio and photo up yesterday and already has 16 women emailing him interested in talking/meeting, etc. That's the good news.

The bad news: I've agreed to meet him tonight because, as he writes, "I've printed out all of their emails, bios and photos and sorted them into piles of yes, no and maybe. Hoping I can review with you."

From: Shelley Manning – May 10, 2011 – 1:15 PM
To: Renee Greene
Subject: Re: Certifiable, no?

16 women interested in Finlay? I'm shocked. Completely shocked. Didn't realize there were that many desperate ladies in LA. What's less shocking is that he's "sorted them" into piles and needs to review them with you. What is his problem?!? What made you agree to reviewing Finlay's Fans?

From: Renee Greene – May 10, 2011 – 1:28 PM
To: Shelley Manning
Subject: Re: Certifiable, no?

Well, if I recall correctly, you hooked up with him, no?

And, he asked if I was free before I understood why he wanted to meet. But honestly, I think this will be fun. Kind of intrigued to see what women are saying to attract his interest.

From: Shelley Manning – May 10, 2011 – 1:36 PM
To: Renee Greene
Subject: Re: Certifiable, no?

That was low, sweetie. You're lucky I love you. Otherwise, that would be grounds for dissolution of the friendship.

Regarding your plans for tonight, I think we have different ideas of what "fun" is. But, I'm kind of curious to hear what types of SOBER women are interested in Finlay. You'll give me the scoop later.

From: Renee Greene – May 10, 2011 – 1:42 PM
To: Shelley Manning
Subject: Re: Certifiable, no?

Sorry. Couldn't resist. Seriously, Mark is a great guy. He's smart, successful, good looking. He just happens to be a bit…particular…about certain things.

From: Shelley Manning – May 10, 2011 – 1:43 PM
To: Renee Greene
Subject: Re: Certifiable, no?

The boy is so anal!

From: Renee Greene – May 10, 2011 – 1:44 PM
To: Shelley Manning
Subject: Re: Certifiable, no?

And…

From: Shelley Manning – May 10, 2011 – 1:44 PM
To: Renee Greene
Subject: Re: Certifiable, no?

And…What?

From: Renee Greene – May 10, 2011 – 1:45 PM
To: Shelley Manning
Subject: Re: Certifiable, no?

I'm waiting for you to say you like anal.

From: Shelley Manning – May 10, 2011 – 1:47 PM
To: Renee Greene
Subject: Re: Certifiable, no?

Renee Michele Greene! I cannot believe you just said that. I'm floored. You have such a dirty mind. Where have you been hiding it and can it come out to play more often?

From: Renee Greene – May 10, 2011 – 1:49 PM
To: Shelley Manning
Subject: Re: Certifiable, no?

I guess I've just been spending too much time with you.

From: Renee Greene – May 11, 2011 – 12:18 AM
To: Shelley Manning
Subject: Exhaustion

I'm exhausted. You know I love Mark. But, this was pure insanity. Sixteen women emailed him and he just picked them apart. Now granted, I did ding one of them for having a ton of typos in her email. I mean, come on. A run on sentence is one thing, but do a basic spell check, would ya?

Even I was embarrassed for her. But, the rest of them seemed really cute, smart, funny and nice. He found something wrong with each and every one of them, with one exception. He's going to email her back today. She's a paralegal going to law school at night. He liked her ambition. Hopefully he'll have better luck than I've been having. Night! Night!

From: Shelley Manning – May 12, 2011 – 8:43 AM
To: Renee Greene
Subject: Re: Exhaustion

I'll bet you a drink at Flint's he finds something out about her via email or on the phone and never goes out with her.

From: Renee Greene – May 12, 2011 – 10:09 AM
To: Shelley Manning
Subject: Re: Exhaustion

You're on!

From: Shelley Manning – May 12, 2011 – 10:10 AM
To: Renee Greene
Subject: Re: Exhaustion

Sucker!

From: Renee Greene – May 12, 2011 – 10:11 AM
To: Shelley Manning
Subject: Re: Exhaustion

Was about to say the same to you.

From: meet@choosejews.com/Patrick41782 – May 13, 2011 – 6:02 PM
To: meet@choosejews.com/PRGal1981
Subject: PR Gal Meet PR Guy!

PR Gal? I'm a PR Guy. Yes, I know. Not many straight guys in PR, but here I am. I work in-house for a large real estate conglomerate. I have my MBA/Masters of Communications joint degree from Pepperdine and was hoping to get into development, but the only opening was in marketing. Would love to meet up and swap stories.

From: meet@choosejews.com/PRGal1981 – May 14, 2011 – 9:26 AM
To: meet@choosejews.com/ Patrick41782
Subject: Re: PR Gal Meet PR Guy!

Hi PR Guy. Yes, you are an anomaly. I have a friend that got her MBA from Pepperdine. Her name is Naomi Franklin. Do you know her?

Well, I've been with a large PR firm for about 8 years, so believe me, I have stories to swap. I'm open to meeting for a drink. I have a client event on Wednesday. What about Thursday?

From: meet@choosejews.com/Patrick41782 – May 14, 2011 – 10:36 AM
To: meet@choosejews.com/PRGal1981
Subject: Re: PR Gal Meet PR Guy!

Thursday is great. Want to say 7:00? Do you know Bandanas on Wilshire? And, I don't know Naomi. When did she graduate?

From: meet@choosejews.com/PRGal1981 – May 14, 2011 – 11:02 AM
To: meet@choosejews.com/ Patrick41782
Subject: Re: PR Gal Meet PR Guy!

YES! Great cole slaw. Sounds perfect. I'll see you then.

p.s. Naomi graduated in 2005.

From: Renee Greene – May 18, 2011 – 6:00 PM
To: Shelley Manning; Mark Finlay
Subject: Date with a PR Guy…Really!

Keep on file – going on a date with a PR guy named Patrick. We're meeting at Bandanas at 7:00 tomorrow night. If I don't call or email later that night – assemble the troops. Oh, and this guy Patrick went to school at Pepperdine, but doesn't know Naomi. Too bad. She always has good scoop on people. Night! Night!

From: Renee Greene – May 19, 2011 – 8:56 PM
To: Shelley Manning; Mark Finlay
Subject: DATE FROM HELL!

Well, we can add tonight's date to the "Dates from Hell" Hall of Fame. It started out fine. I got there a few minutes early to find a place at the bar and make sure the light was hitting me on my good side. He walked in and looked exactly like his picture. That's always a plus. We ordered drinks and started talking about work stuff. Even though he works in house, we had similar experiences dealing with media and various personalities. Everything is humming along nicely, great conversation, etc. when all of the sudden a waitress walks over and this is what transpires.

> Waitress: "Patrick, what are you doing here?"
>
> Patrick: "I didn't know you were still working here. I'm here with Renee. Renee, this is Maggie."
>
> Me: "Hi Maggie. Nice to meet you."
>
> Maggie: "What the fuck, Patrick? You shouldn't be here."
>
> Patrick: "Really, I heard you took a job someplace else. I didn't know you would be here."
>
> Maggie: "Right. I don't believe you. If you think coming in here with some skank is going to make me jealous, you're wrong. I want you to leave me alone. I think you should leave…now!"
>
> Me: "Actually, I'm going to leave."

UGH! Apparently, he thought being seen with me was going to make his ex jealous. And what the #$@%? (Excuse my language!) A skank? I will have you know I came straight from work. It's not like I showed up with some short skirt and stiletto heels. I was wearing a pant suit, for gosh sakes.

From: Shelley Manning – May 19, 2011 – 10:07 PM
To: Renee Greene; Mark Finlay
Subject: Re: DATE FROM HELL!

:(Lunch tomorrow at Mel's? I'll wear something slutty so you look less like a skank.

From: Renee Greene – May 19, 2011 – 11:02 PM
To: Shelley Manning; Mark Finlay
Subject: Re: DATE FROM HELL!

Perfect! See you tomorrow for a wine and whine-filled lunch.

From: Mark Finlay – May 20, 2011 – 1:14 AM
To: Shelley Manning; Renee Greene
Subject: Re: DATE FROM HELL!

Skanks and sluts? Not sure I want to continue getting cc'd on all of these emails. Oh hell, who I am kidding? These are the highlight of my code-writing day. Ha! Ha!

From: meet@choosejews.com/TaxTime2002 – May 24, 2011 – 7:03 PM
To: meet@choosejews.com/PRGal1981
Subject: Ready for some fun

Hi. I'm Michael, an easy-going CPA and tax season is…finally…over. I enjoy riding bikes along the beach, seeing movies, checking out the latest food trucks and watching tennis on TV. Looking for a fun, genuine gal to hang out with and really appreciate honesty and a good sense of humor. I'm not overly religious, but finding someone Jewish is important to me. If you think you fit the bill, would love to meet up for dinner. Let me know what you think.

From: meet@choosejews.com/PRGal1981 – May 25, 2011 - 10:07 AM
To: meet@choosejews.com/TaxTime2002
Subject: Re: Ready for some fun

Congratulations on surviving tax season. I imagine that must be like running a marathon every day for a month – or more.

Looking at your profile, it seems like we do have a lot in common. Why don't you give me a call and we can talk more? My number is 310.555.2187.

From: Renee Greene – May 27, 2011 – 11:26 AM
To: Mark Finlay
Subject: Paralegal Update?

Hey there. Didn't want to ask you at Flint's last night in front of everyone. What is up with you and the paralegal you met online? Do tell. Do tell. Do tell.

From: Mark Finlay – May 27, 2011 – 5:05 PM
To: Renee Greene
Subject: Re: Paralegal Update?

Thanks for your discretion. Not that I'm embarrassed to be doing the online dating thing. I just don't want everybody (READ: SHELLEY!) knowing my business. Long story short – unlike you, I actually know how to make a long story short ;) – I googled her and found some inappropriate photos of her online. Looks as though she is saving money for law school by doing something risqué on the side. So, I called it off.

From: Renee Greene – May 28, 2011 – 9:13 AM
To: Mark Finlay
Subject: Re: Paralegal Update?

Oh, I can see why that would be a deal breaker for you. How many dates had you gone on? Not to get too personal, but had you slept with her? How did she take it?

From: Mark Finlay – May 28, 2011 – 3:20 PM
To: Renee Greene
Subject: Re: Paralegal Update?

This was a few days before our first date. I just told her that work was getting crazy, deadlines were looming and that it just wouldn't be fair to her to start something that I knew I wouldn't be able to devote time to.

From: Renee Greene – May 28, 2011 – 3:50 PM
To: Mark Finlay
Subject: Re: Paralegal Update?

Ah, the old "I'm too busy with work" excuse. I'm quite familiar with it.

From: Mark Finlay – May 28, 2011 – 3:52 PM
To: Renee Greene
Subject: Re: Paralegal Update?

Oh, come on now. I was letting her down gently. I never would have said that if we had slept together.

From: Renee Greene – May 28, 2011 – 3:55 PM
To: Mark Finlay
Subject: Re: Paralegal Update?

I know. I'm still just reeling over what a complete ASS Matt turned out to be and what a SUCKER I turned out to be. I know you're one of the good ones. I'll call you later.

From: Renee Greene – May 28, 2011 – 4:07 PM
To: Shelley Manning
Subject: Winner Winner Chicken Dinner

Oh yeah, forgot to tell you, Mark never went out with that paralegal chick. He found some racy photos of her online and that was a deal breaker. So, you win the bet. I'll buy you a drink tonight at Flint's? And, please don't say anything to Mark. He doesn't want anyone to know about his online dating escapades.

From: Shelley Manning – May 28, 2011 – 4:22 PM
To: Renee Greene
Subject: Re: Winner Winner Chicken Dinner

HA! I KNEW IT! Yes, I will collect a Flint's special mojito tonight. See you there. Mwah! Mwah!

From: Renee Greene – May 31, 2011 – 4:07 PM
To: Shelley Manning; Mark Finlay
Subject: Tax-adermy

Just giving you the 411 in writing on my upcoming date with Michael – an accountant. Per the subject of my email, let's hope he's more LIVELY than one would typically expect from an accountant. We're going to Bamboo Garden on Friday.

From: Shelley Manning – May 31, 2011 – 5:53 PM
To: Renee Greene
Subject: Re: Tax-adermy

So noted. But, I wouldn't object to you getting a little stuffed, if you know what I mean. A little stuffing would do you some good.

From: Renee Greene – May 31, 2011 – 6:05 PM
To: Shelley Manning
Subject: Re: Tax-adermy

Yes, we all know you're a big fan of both the "stuff" and "stuffing." I'll keep you posted.

From: Mark Finlay – May 31, 2011 – 8:29 PM
To: Renee Greene; Shelley Manning
Subject: Re: Tax-adermy

Bamboo Garden? Smart man. Get the mu shu chicken for me. Be careful and call me when you get home. I'll be up.

From: Renee Greene – June 4, 2010 – 12:07 AM
To: Shelley Manning
Subject: Home SWEET Home

Hey Shelley. Made it home safely. Michael seems like a really great guy. I met him at Bamboo Garden (his suggestion, so there's one thing in his favor). We had great conversation at dinner and then ended up taking a drive in his car through Mulholland.

Yes, I know. Broke a cardinal rule of online dating by getting into his car. But, he seemed totally normal, so I thought it would be okay. We parked the car, got in the backseat and made out for an hour like a couple of horny teenagers. (I figured you would approve!)
Then he drove me back to my car, gave me a sweet kiss goodnight and said he hoped we could do it again. Aha! A date that didn't go horribly awry. I'm proceeding with extreme caution. But trying to be optimistic. I feel like a tightrope walker in the circus. Know what I mean?

From: Shelley Manning – June 4, 2011 – 11:08 AM
To: Renee Greene
Subject: Re: Home SWEET Home

Horny teenager, indeed. That's so awesome.

I've been acting like a horny teenager myself lately with a young gentleman we'll call Slippery Pete. He's the "love 'em and leave 'em" type, that slips out as fast as he can, unlike the Cuddler who just wants to hang out all night long. Believe me, I love it when they "come" and then go. So, are you going to email this horny teenager or wait to hear from him first?

From: Renee Greene – June 4, 2011 – 1:45 PM
To: Shelley Manning
Subject: Re: Home SWEET Home

Yes, kick those cuddlers to the curb! (But be gentle; you don't want to make them cry.) I'm going to wait until Monday to email Michael. Don't want to come across as desperate or anything.

From: Shelley Manning – June 4, 2011 – 1:48 PM
To: Renee Greene
Subject: Re: Home SWEET Home

Good idea. Keep me posted! Mwah! Mwah!

From: meet@choosejews.com/TaxTime2002 – June 6, 2011 – 9:36 AM
To: meet@choosejews.com/PRGal1981
Subject: GREAT Time!

Hey there! Had a great time with you Friday night. The conversation was so easy and natural. And, making out in the backseat of the car wasn't too shabby either. Felt like I was 16 again. You're a great kisser.

I must say, it is so wonderful to finally meet a generous, warm-hearted, smart, funny and beautiful woman. I can already tell how special you are. Would love to see you again. What does next week look like for you?

From: meet@choosejews.com/TaxTime2002 – June 6 – 9:38 AM
To: meet@choosejews.com/PRGal1981
Subject: GREAT Time!

Hey there! Had a great time with you Saturday night. The conversation was so easy and natural. And, making out in the backseat of the car wasn't too shabby either. Felt like I was 16 again. You're a great kisser.

I must say, it is so wonderful to finally meet a generous, warm-hearted, smart, funny and beautiful woman. I can already tell how special you are. Would love to see you again. What does next week look like for you?

From: Renee Greene – June 6 – 9:56 AM
To: Shelley Manning
Subject: Fwd: GREAT Time! – Email One of Two

See below…and await my next forwarded message

From: Renee Greene – June 6 – 9:56 AM
To: Shelley Manning
Subject: Fwd: GREAT Time! – Email Two of Two

What the #$@%? Are you kidding me?!?!

Okay, so we went on ONE date. I get that I can't expect that he would not be seeing anyone else. But, to send the EXACT same email to two DIFFERENT women from the SAME weekend. EW! That's just gross.

From: Shelley Manning – June 6 – 11:56 AM
To: Renee Greene
Subject: Re: Fwd: GREAT Time! – Email Two of Two

I'm totally with you. What a douche bag! What are you going to do? Email back? Ignore him?

From: meet@choosejews.com/PRGal1981 – June 6 – 12:25 PM
To: meet@choosejews.com/TaxTime2002
Bcc: Shelley Manning
Subject: Re: GREAT Time!

Hi Michael. I must say, I was so flattered to see your email. I felt so LUCKY to have met such a NICE, DECENT and HONEST guy. It truly made ME feel special until…

From: meet@choosejews.com/PRGal1981 – June 6 – 12:32 PM
To: meet@choosejews.com/TaxTime2002
Bcc: Shelley Manning
Subject: Re: GREAT Time!

…I got your next email.

Then I realized how lucky YOU are to have met two "generous, warm-hearted, smart, funny and beautiful women" – and on the SAME WEEKEND! I can't imagine how difficult this must be for YOU to juggle two such amazing gals who are BOTH great kissers. So, being the "generous" woman that I am, I will make this very easy for you. Buh-by!

From: Shelley Manning – June 6 – 12:54 PM
To: Renee Greene
Subject: Re: GREAT Time!

Love it! Love it! Love it! You are my new hero and getting great at this whole online rejection thing.

From: Renee Greene – June 6 – 12:58 PM
To: Shelley Manning
Subject: Re: GREAT Time!

What, I'm getting good at being rejected by losers, lame-ohs, cheaters and scumbags I've met online?

From: Shelley Manning – June 6 – 1:26 PM
To: Renee Greene
Subject: Re: GREAT Time!

No. You know what I mean. You are getting great at telling people off. I've said for a long time that you need to stand up for yourself more. And, I think being able to say it like it is without having to say it to their faces is making you the brave woman I've always known was lurking in that chocolate chip cookie-baking, non-confrontational, big-hearted gal. You know I'm your biggest fan!

From: meet@choosejews.com/PartyPete – June 9, 2011 – 2:38 PM
To: meet@choosejews.com/PRGal1981
Subject: You sound fun

Hi there. I just saw your profile and think you sound fun. I'm Pete – an outgoing, energetic guy who works in sales. My motto is work hard/play hard and nothing is more important to me than my friends and family. I would love to meet up for a drink sometime and get to know one another. Let me know what you think.

From: meet@choosejews.com/PRGal1981 – June 10, 2011 – 9:18 AM
To: meet@choosejews.com/PartyPete
Subject: Re: You sound fun

Hi Pete. I'm all about family and friends too. A drink sounds fun. What did you have in mind?

From: meet@choosejews.com/PartyPete – June 10, 2011 – 10:31 AM
To: meet@choosejews.com/PRGal1981
Subject: Re: You sound fun

Do you know Rachel's in Santa Monica? They have GREAT margaritas (if that's your thing). Maybe Thursday after work – say 7:00? I'll be able to find you. Those dimples in your photo are hard to miss.

From: meet@choosejews.com/PRGal1981 – June 10, 2011 – 11:12 AM
To: meet@choosejews.com/PartyPete
Subject: Re: You sound fun

I haven't been to Rachel's before, but I do love a good margarita. Thursday at 7:00 sounds perfect. See you then.

From: Renee Greene – June 16, 2011 – 9:45 AM
To: Shelley Manning; Mark Finlay
Subject: Margaritas with Pete

I'm meeting a guy named Pete at Rachel's tonight for a margarita at 7:00. I'll call or email when I get home.

From: Renee Greene – June 16, 2011 – 10:42 PM
To: Shelley Manning
Subject: I need a drink!

UGH! Pete Greenwald is NOT the man for me. Every story started with, "My buddies and I were out drinking one night…" And when I say every story, I mean EVERY story. So, when you start talking about the good ol' college days, you expect there to be a few anecdotes where you and your "buddies" are out knocking back a few cold ones.
But, something came up about parents and he confided that his mom was killed in a car accident a few years ago. I responded with a genuine and sympathetic "I'm so sorry. That's just horrible." And he said, "Yeah. It really sucked. My buddies and I were out drinking one night…" and I just tuned out from there. UGH! UGH! UGH!

From: Shelley Manning – June 17, 2011 – 8:12 AM
To: Renee Greene
Subject: Re: I need a drink!

Perhaps his buddies have to drink all the time because they need *something* to get them through a night of Pete's stories? Don't despair, sweetie! Your dream man is out there. I promise.

I, on the other hand, could use a drink. I hooked up last night with a guy we will refer to as "Wee Man." And no, this isn't a joke about the size of his junk. This has to do with the fact he was turned on by the thought of being urinated on. YUCK! Maybe it's time for me to settle down.

From: Renee Greene – June 17, 2011 – 8:26 AM
To: Shelley Manning
Subject: Re: I need a drink!

What?!? You settle down? Blasphemy. You're "pissing" me off with talk like that.

From: Shelley Manning – June 17, 2011 – 8:29 AM
To: Renee Greene
Subject: Re: I need a drink!

HA! A "Wee Man" pun. Nice! Not as good as all of the Cuddler jokes, but good nonetheless. Can always count on you for a laugh.

From: Renee Greene – June 19, 2011 – 9:09 AM
To: Ashley Price
Subject: Everything Okay

Hey there. Just wanted to email to see if everything was okay. I left you a message a few days ago and haven't heard back. I know you were going to Chicago for work, but I thought you would be back by now. Just worried and miss you friend.

From: Ashley Price – June 21, 2011 – 1:13 PM
To: Renee Greene
Subject: Re: Everything Okay

Sorry. Yes, I got back from Chicago on Saturday morning. Meant to call you back but got wrapped up in things with Evan. We had a really great Saturday night and then got in a stupid argument about him getting a haircut on Sunday. It started out with an innocent question by me about why he always cuts it so short and wouldn't it look better if he let it grow out a bit. From there it escalated into World War III about how I never support him in anything. It was pretty awful. So, I've just spent the past few days wallowing in self pity and drowning my sorrows in cupcakes.

From: Renee Greene – June 21, 2011 – 2:02 PM
To: Ashley Price
Subject: Re: Everything Okay

I'm so sorry. I know you're probably not up for meeting at Flint's. Want to just grab a quiet dinner and talk?

From: Ashley Price – June 21, 2011 – 2:05 PM
To: Renee Greene
Subject: Re: Everything Okay

That would be great. I'll call you tomorrow and we'll set something up.

From: meet@choosejews.com/AdMan922 – June 22, 2011 – 9:02 AM
To: meet@choosejews.com/PRGal1981
Subject: Adorable

I love how you modestly acknowledged in your profile how other people would describe you. I would say…adorable!

From: Renee Greene – June 22, 2011 – 9:32 AM
To: Shelley Manning
Subject: Fwd: Adorable

<blush!>

From: Shelley Manning – June 22, 2011 – 9:51 AM
To: Renee Greene
Subject: Re: Fwd: Adorable

That is very sweet. What's his story? Is he cute? Are you going to go out with him?

From: Renee Greene – June 22, 2011 – 9:58 AM
To: Shelley Manning
Subject: Re: Fwd: Adorable

Honestly, I haven't logged in to his profile yet. But, unless he's got a massive facial deformity or lists his profession as serial killer, I have to meet this guy. *He* sounds adorable.

From: Shelley Manning – June 22, 2011 – 10:02 AM
To: Renee Greene
Subject: Re: Fwd: Adorable

Well, stop emailing me and email him. Sheesh!

From: meet@choosejews.com/PRGal1981 – June 22, 2011 – 10:15 AM
To: meet@choosejews.com/AdMan922
Bcc: Shelley Manning
Subject: Re: Adorable

Thank you for that sweet introduction. I must confess, I blushed a bit. I hope you don't think this is too forward, but would you like to meet for a drink or something?

From: meet@choosejews.com/AdMan922 – June 22, 2011 – 7:35 PM
To: meet@choosejews.com/PRGal1981
Bcc: Shelley Manning
Subject: Re: Adorable

Are you up for dinner? I noticed from your profile that you like Italian food. Have you ever been to Emilio's on Pico? What about Sunday night at 8:00?

From: Shelley Manning – June 22, 2011 – 8:15 PM
To: Renee Greene
Subject: Fwd: Re: Adorable

He read your profile. That's a good sign. Not only is he interested in you, but he reads too. ;)

From: Renee Greene – June 22, 2011 – 8:15 PM
To: Shelley Manning
Subject: Re: Fwd: Re: Adorable

HA!

From: meet@choosejews.com/PRGal1981 – June 23, 2011 – 9:01 AM
To: meet@choosejews.com/AdMan922
Bcc: Shelley Manning
Subject: Re: Adorable

Sunday at 8:00 at Emilio's sounds great. I will see you there.

From: Renee Greene – June 23, 2011 – 9:03 AM
To: Mark Finlay
Subject: Date Alert!

I have a date on Sunday with Mike at Emilio's at 8:00. I'll call you when I get home.

From: Mark Finlay – June 23, 2011 – 10:12 AM
To: Renee Greene
Subject: Date Alert!

Mmmmm! Love Emilio's. Enjoy, enjoy, enjoy.

From: Renee Greene – June 26, 2011 – 11:02 PM
To: Shelley Manning
Subject: Honey? Snap, snap!

You know I've always said you can tell a lot about a person on how they treat other people. This guy could not have been nicer…to me. But, he could not have been more of a – excuse my language, here – dick to the waitress. Anytime he needing something, he kept snapping his fingers at her and calling her honey – or just hon. I was so embarrassed. I just kept looking at her with these sympathetic eyes and she kept looking at me in horror. It was just awful.

From: Shelley Manning – June 27, 2011 – 8:52 AM
To: Renee Greene
Subject: Re: Honey? Snap, snap!

I hate, hate, hate when guys call you honey. You know what honey is? It's bee excretion.

From: Renee Greene – June 27, 2011 – 9:47 AM
To: Shelley Manning
Subject: Re: Honey? Snap, snap!

Ha! Ha! Thank you for taking a crap evening and making it so that I can laugh about it at the end of the day. I'll call you later, hon.

From: Shelley Manning – June 27, 2011 – 10:17 AM
To: Renee Greene
Subject: Re: Honey? Snap, snap!

Don't call me bee shit! ;) Mwah! Mwah!

From: Ashley Price – June 28, 2011 – 2:01 AM
To: Renee Greene
Subject: Bitter Party of One

No. That's not a new brand of strong coffee. But wouldn't that be a GREAT name? I know. I know. I've been MIA for a while. Sorry. Things with Evan have been…rocky to say the least. We had this big fight…again…where he told me I'm a snobby, judgmental person who is always on his case about being an underachiever. Before you say anything, I know. I'm too good for him. So, you'll be happy to know we've called it quits.

I could really use an ice cream sundae from Mel's to drown my sorrows and lament the fact I will end up alone. It's got to be better than succumbing to the indignity of online dating or the bar scene – no offense to you or Shelley (well, maybe a bit of an aside to her). Anyway, call me tomorrow.

From: meet@choosejews.com/GreenLife66 – June 28, 2011 – 8:29 PM
To: meet@choosejews.com/PRGal1981
Subject: Liked your profile

Hi there. My name is Andrew and I really liked reading your profile.
I'm a salesman for a company that makes green cleaning products. Not that I'm obsessed with the environment or anything. And not that I don't care about it either.

Anyway, you're my very first email and I think I'm a bit nervous. Hoping you won't hold that against me and that maybe we could have a drink. Let me know. Thanks.

From: meet@choosejews.com/PRGal1981 – June 29, 2011 – 9:23 AM
To: meet@choosejews.com/GreenLife66
Subject: Re: Liked your profile

Hi Andrew. No worries about being a bit nervous and welcome to this strange new world known as online dating. I imagine it must be a nice feeling to know that what you do is not harming the planet. I work in PR and sometimes think we spend too much time and energy stressing out about things that are pretty inconsequential. We joke, it's PR not ER. Anyway, why don't we meet up for a coffee? How does Sunday afternoon sound? I'm in West LA. What about you?

From: meet@choosejews.com/GreenLife66 – June 29, 2011 – 10:08 AM
To: meet@choosejews.com/PRGal1981
Subject: Re: Liked your profile

Sunday sounds good. I'm downtown, but could easily meet you in Westwood. How does 11:00 sound at the Coffee World?

From: meet@choosejews.com/PRGal1981 – June 29, 2011 – 10:26 AM
To: meet@choosejews.com/GreenLife66
Subject: Re: Liked your profile

Don't want to be difficult, but can we meet somewhere else instead. Say, Juice Joint? I don't drink coffee. See you Sunday?

From: meet@choosejews.com/GreenLife66 – June 29, 2011 – 11:06 AM
To: meet@choosejews.com/PRGal1981
Subject: Re: Liked your profile

Sounds good.

From: Renee Greene – July 3, 2011 – 10:05 AM
To: Shelley Manning; Mark Finlay
Subject: Collide with my date?

On my way to Juice Joint to meet Andrew. He works for an environmental products company. But, I get the sense he's no "EarthMan." If you're around – stop by. Would be fun for you to "bump" into us.

From: Renee Greene – July 3, 2011 – 1:59 PM
To: Shelley Manning; Mark Finlay
Subject: What a difference an apostrophe makes

Okay, met this guy for a juice this morning and he was SMOKING. No, not SMOKIN'. SMOKING!

His profile said "non-smoker" and mine said "non-smoker" but he was smoking! It started out just fine. He arrived and was really cute in a boyish way. He was really nervous, but it came across as totally genuine and sweet. I ordered a blended (of course) and he ordered an iced coffee. We also decided to split a chocolate chip twist. When I reached for my wallet, he was almost offended. Again, not in a bad way, but in a really sweet way. Then he asked if I minded if we sat outside. It was a bit cool for me, but I said sure. We started talking and he's really…sweet. Yes, I know I've said sweet about a gazillion times already, but it truly is the best way to describe him.

Then, out of nowhere, he lights up. And, he didn't even ask if I minded if he smoked. He just lit up. First off, it was so disgusting! But, even more so, it seemed so odd to me that he was so sweet – yes, I know, sweet again – and he didn't even bother to ask if the smoking would bother me. I didn't even know what to say. So, I just kept on with the date. But afterward, when he walked me back to my car and leaned in for a kiss, I had to draw the line. I told him that I thought he was really sweet (UGH! I need a thesaurus or something) but that I don't date smokers. He said he's not really a smoker, but just likes an occasional cigarette. I told him that I was going to have to pass – that even the occasional smoker wasn't going to work for me. It was horribly awkward.

From: Mark Finlay – July 3, 2011 – 2:30 PM
To: Shelley Manning; Renee Greene
Subject: Re: What a difference an apostrophe makes

Note taken. Smoking bad. Smokin' good. And, will make a note that you need a thesaurus for Channukah. Yes, it's six months away, but you know I like to plan ahead. Hang in there!!

From: Shelley Manning – July 5, 2011 – 8:02 AM
To: Renee Greene
Subject: Re: What a difference an apostrophe makes

Sorry I wasn't able to swing by, sweetie. And, sorry I've not emailed back for a day or two. I was busy celebrating Independence Day making some fireworks. We'll refer to this guy as The Rocket from now on. He was quite explosive.

As far as your date went: Smokin' – yes. Smoking – no. So sorry, Renee. But I must say I'm quite proud of you for dealing with confrontation head on and in person during the KISS GOODBYE and not resorting to an email to give him the KISS OFF. While the man of your dreams must still be out there, I think this has been a good experience for you so far.

From: Renee Greene – July 5, 2011 – 10:42 AM
To: Shelley Manning
Subject: Re: What a difference an apostrophe makes

Well, I'm delighted to hear you think it's been a good experience so far. I think it's been depressing, horrifying, embarrassing, pointless and demoralizing. Guess I don't need a thesaurus after all. ;) But, what I do need is a break….and perhaps a good cuddle (HA! HA!) Meet at Mel's tomorrow for lunch – usual time.

From: Renee Greene – July 5, 2011 – 10:45 AM
To: member.services@choosejews.com
Subject: Profile on Hold

I was writing to request that you please hide my profile from viewing until further notice. My ID# is 49628; Screen Name: PRGal1981.

From: member.services@choosejews.com – July 5, 2011 – 10:48 AM
To: Renee Greene
Subject: Re: Profile on Hold

Profile has been hidden until further request.

CHAPTER 6: DATING THE OLD-FASHIONED WAY

From: Renee Greene – July 11, 2011 – 11:37 AM
To: Shelley Manning, Ashley Price, Mark Finlay
Subject: Drum Roll Please…

You will never believe this. After years of toiling away on boring corporate and consumer products (let me tell you, I've literally watched the paint dry on behalf of Excel Paint), I'm *finally* getting an assignment that literally ROCKS. We just got hired to help Nuvision with the launch of a new video game. Our first project is to help them with an event they are sponsoring with MTV in a few short weeks. A bunch of pro extreme athletes will be there. And, Marsh 7 will be performing. While they aren't my favorite – can you imagine if it were Spider Fire! – I'm still excited to see them perform live...and for work no less. We're hosting the green room for all of the VIPs, so I'll be hob nobbing with the celebs. Much work to do before then, but wanted to share the exciting news. Hurrah!

From: Mark Finlay – July 11, 2011 – 12:22 PM
To: Renee Greene
Subject: Re: Drum Roll Please…

Nuvision? Those greedy corporate shills? Just kidding. I know a bunch of guys that work over there. It's a good shop. They are lucky to have you representing them. Only wish my little ol' company could afford the amazing PR prowess of one, Ms. Renee Greene. Glad to know you are finally getting to do something fun and worthy of your wonderful charms.

From: Renee Greene – July 11, 2011 – 12:23 PM
To: Mark Finlay
Subject: Re: Drum Roll Please…

<blush>

From: Shelley Manning – July 11, 2011 – 2:56 PM
To: Renee Greene
Subject: Re: Drum Roll Please…

That is so cool. So you aren't a huge fan, but you are right. Exciting just to be there. I can't wait to hear all about the celebs and stars. Those extreme athletes are really hot, too. My friend Cheryl went to the X Games and said they have really taut bodies. I guess hurling your body up a ramp while standing on a piece of plywood with a few wheels strapped on really gets your legs, abs and buns in shape. Yum!

From: Renee Greene – July 11, 2011 – 4:55 PM
To: Shelley Manning
Subject: Re: Drum Roll Please…

So I guess that you are the S (for Shelley) that adds SEX to EXtreme. UGH! That was totally lame. I realized as I was writing it that I was trying to be clever and basically, it just isn't working. But, rather than erase it, I thought I would show you that I've at least made an effort. Loser, huh?

From: Shelley Manning – July 11, 2011 – 5:07 PM
To: Renee Greene
Subject: Re: Drum Roll Please…

You are NOT a loser. Granted that was lame. Very lame.

But I don't want to hear this loser bullshit. You are always so down on yourself. You are amazing, wonderful, smart, talented, terrific. So get over yourself and just accept it. YOU rock. YOU are SUPERMODEL RENEE!!!

From: Renee Greene – July 11, 2011 – 6:32 PM
To: Shelley Manning
Subject: Re: Drum Roll Please…

Sorry. I know I have this bad habit of always putting myself down. Bad habits are hard to break. Thanks for always being such an incredibly supportive friend and for giving me a good kick in the ass when I need it.

From: Renee Greene – July 12, 2011 – 11:31 PM
To: Shelley Manning
Subject: Douche Bag Alert!

Where are you? It's 11:30 on a Tuesday. I tried calling because I was having a bad moment and logged on to the dating site to look at Matt's photo. I know totally lame. Can we say Cyber Stalker? So I'm looking through his profile and that jerk took material from my "you're an ass" email and put it into his profile. He basically stole my "I deserve" speech and made it sound like that's who HE IS. I'm so mad right now I could literally scream. HELP!

From: Shelley Manning – July 13, 2011 – 9:31 AM
To: Renee Greene
Subject: Re: Douche Bag Alert!

Sorry!!!!!!!!!

Was out late last night. Had a wild date with this guy I met at a party last weekend. The Tongue, as he will be known moving forward, was quite a talent. Quite the talent indeed.

Anyway, I'm sorry I wasn't there when you called. What an absolutely miserable scuz bucket. I cannot believe that he did that.

Call me tonight. I'll be home around 7:00 and you can scream all you want. Mwah! Mwah!

From: Shelley Manning – July 14, 2011 – 11:22 AM
To: Renee Greene
Subject: Wanna Smoke a Long One?

Ha! That is not code for anything. Shocking, I know. Hey, I know it's short notice, but I got invited to this swanky, private cigar bar in Beverly Hills tomorrow night. Want to come along? The Tongue is bringing a couple of friends. Could be fun? And maybe if we get lucky – or should I say the guys get lucky – there will be something illicit happening. :)

From: Renee Greene – July 14, 2011 – 7:02 PM
To: Shelley Manning
Subject: Re: Wanna Smoke a Long One?

Sorry for my delay in responding. Was at a client meeting all day and just getting home. While I'm sure The Tongue has some friends that would make delightful company, I'm just not up for meeting anyone right now. I'm much happier wallowing in self pity with a can of frosting. Don't be mad.

From: Shelley Manning – July 15, 2011 – 10:32 AM
To: Renee Greene
Subject: Re: Wanna Smoke a Long One?

You have pretty much been through the ringer, which is why I thought a night at an exclusive club would be a nice treat. But, if you would rather sulk, I get it. Let's plan to meet for brunch on Sunday around 11ish. Sound good?

From: Renee Greene – July 15, 2011 – 10:35 AM
To: Shelley Manning
Subject: Re: Wanna Smoke a Long One?

Perfect. Have fun.

From: Ashley Price – June 18, 2011 – 2:00 PM
To: Renee Greene
Subject: Why So Glum?

You sounded so glum on the phone. Don't give me this "I don't feel like talking" business. What's up?

From: Renee Greene – June 18, 2011 – 2:30 PM
To: Ashley Price
Subject: Re: Why So Glum?

Ugh! Well, a few months ago, I met this guy Matt through the online dating site and foolishly fell for his charms. After he slept with me, he dumped me.

I responded with a dignified email that told him what a royal shit he is and how I deserve better. Just found out he took the "I deserve" part and re-did his profile using all of the information to make it sound like he *is* this really great guy. I'm just in a self-pitying funk. Nothing a few more cans of frosting won't cure. Sorry I was so curt on the phone. I know you were just checking in. Hope you are well. Let's make some plans to meet at Mel's when I'm back from Vegas.

From: Ashley Price – June 18, 2011 – 4:45 PM
To: Renee Greene
Subject: Re: Why So Glum?

So sorry to hear that Renee. You do deserve better! And, honestly it's no surprise someone you met online turned out to be full of complete crap. Yes on Mel's. Call me when you're back and we'll put it on the calendar.

From: Renee Greene – June 18, 2011 – 5:02 PM
To: Shelley Manning
Subject: Fwd: Re: Why So Glum?

Why do I always get a sense there's some schadenfreude going on in her emails?

From: Renee Greene – June 19, 2011 – 8:22 AM
To: Shelley Manning
Subject: Re: Fwd: Re: Why So Glum?

Schaden-what?

From: Renee Greene – June 19, 2011 – 8:35 AM
To: Shelley Manning
Subject: Re: Fwd: Re: Why So Glum?

Schadenfreude. It's a German word that means other people are taking pleasure in your misery.

From: Shelley Manning – June 19, 2011 – 8:40 AM
To: Renee Greene
Subject: Re: Fwd: Re: Why So Glum?

Oh, of course, Schadenfreude. I think you sense it because deep down you know she wants everyone else around her to be miserable too. Well, let's just say, I'm the ying to her yang. I want NOTHING but the VERY BEST for you.

From: Renee Greene – June 19, 2011 – 8:45 AM
To: Shelley Manning
Subject: Re: Fwd: Re: Why So Glum?

Thanks!

From: Renee Greene – July 21, 2011 – 9:13 AM
To: Mark Finlay
Subject: Dateless in LA?

I got your voicemail and now fear you are avoiding my return call. ARE YOU KIDDING ME? How can you have not gone on one single cyber date yet? You posted your bio a month and a half ago! And I know you are getting emails. So, what's the deal?!? Send me your password. I am logging on and will find the PERFECT woman for you.

From: Mark Finlay – July 21, 2011 – 9:17 AM
To: Renee Greene
Subject: Re: Dateless in LA?

Yes, I've been avoiding your calls and yes, I haven't gone on a date yet. I knew you'd be angry and you know how I hate to disappoint you. All of these choices are too overwhelming for me. And, I'm totally swamped with work. The password is my birthday – two digit month, day and year. I know. Pretty lame, huh? Just couldn't think of anything else.

From: Renee Greene – July 21, 2011 – 9:27 AM
To: Mark Finlay
Subject: Re: Dateless in LA?

It's not lame. It's easy to remember. Granted, easy for someone to steal, but I doubt anyone is going to log in and set up random dates on your behalf. Okay, my mission for this weekend is to scour the site for your perfect match. I'll be in touch.

From: Renee Greene – July 23, 2011 – 11:28 PM
To: Shelley Manning
Subject: Holy Cow!

HOLY COW! You are NOT going to believe this. I'm home, yes on a Saturday night and yes, you are out doing something probably fun and wild, but I'm home. (That's not the part you aren't going to believe!)

I'm online, looking through dating profiles to find the perfect woman for Mark. Stop laughing. Just because the two of you didn't work out (Tee Hee!), doesn't mean there isn't someone perfect for him out there. As my great grandma used to say, for every seat, there's a tuchus.

So, I start off going through all of the women who have emailed him. And believe me, he's coming across as quite the catch. I emailed back to a few of them and then started my own search. I'm going through scores of women and come across a profile for… ASHLEY! Yes, that Ashley.

After all of that shit she gave me about online dating being for desperate people, she's right there among the pack scouring for love online. What a hypocrite. And to think I felt pretty lame for doing this online thing and here she is on there, too. ARGH! What should I do?!?

From: Shelley Manning – July 25, 2011 – 11:01 AM
To: Renee Greene
Subject: Re: Holy Cow!

Sorry sweetie. Was in bed all weekend. His name was Christian but from now on, he shall be known as Mocha Man. He liked EVERYTHING dipped in chocolate. Yummy!

Anyway, I'm just getting to emails. Gotta confess, I'm not surprised at all that Miss Priss is a hypocrite. Those judgmental types usually are. Just look at all the overly religious folks and bible thumpers who end up sleeping with hookers, doing drugs, and cheating on their wives.

But I digress. First of all, you should NOT be feeling bad or desperate about online dating. Lots of people are doing this these days. In fact, I read that one in five relationships now start online. What you should feel bad about is letting her damage your (sadly and unjustifiably) already ailing self-esteem.

What you need is a big ol' dose of moral superiority and you can get that by calling her out on her behavior and attitude.

From: Renee Greene – July 25, 2011 – 3:03 PM
To: Shelley Manning
Subject: Re: Holy Cow!

You're so right. And just the other day, she said she and Evan called it off because he told her she was a judgmental snob. And, instead of thinking that maybe she has some things to work on, she just said she deserves better than him. Now granted, I keep telling her she deserves better. Evan is an ass and a half, but still. She looks in the mirror and sees right past every flaw but has no problem noticing and pointing out the flaws in everyone else. I'm so pissed right now (Should we call Wee Man? –Tee Hee!) that I could just SCREAM!

From: Shelley Manning – July 25, 2011 – 3:15 PM
To: Renee Greene
Subject: Re: Holy Cow!

Harness that anger, channel it into a coherent but honest tirade and let 'er rip. And, don't forget to call or email me when it's done. I'm SO curious how it goes. Would seriously LOVE to be a fly on the wall for that one.

From: Renee Greene – July 25, 2011 – 9:07 PM
To: Shelley Manning
Subject: Re: Holy Cow!

So I just got off the phone with Ashley and really let her have it. But not before I wrote out a speech on paper so I didn't chicken out.

Basically, I told her that in all of the years we've been friends, I've looked past her snide comments and judgmental behavior because bottom line, she's been a good friend and we've been friends for so long. But I was outraged (yes, I used the word outraged) that she continued to make me feel bad about something and then was doing the same thing behind my back.

She broke down and started crying. But I didn't relent. I held my ground and explained her behavior was unacceptable. She apologized profusely and said that she's just a very insecure person who probably uses it as a defense mechanism. Well, I told her that defense mechanism or not, she needs to be honest and refrain from making unfair judgments or we would have to dissolve our friendship.

I've NEVER spoken to anyone like *that* before in my entire life. I'm literally shaking.

From: Shelley Manning – July 25, 2011 – 10:02 PM
To: Renee Greene
Subject: Re: Holy Cow!

<Jaw drops!> I cannot believe it. You are truly the new Queen of Confrontation. I know that must have been excruciating for you, but I imagine you feel a sense of relief and calm about not holding all of those feelings in. I'm logging off now. Have an early morning meeting. See you at Mel's tomorrow. Mwah! Mwah!

From: Renee Greene – July 29, 2011 – 3:30 PM
To: Shelley Manning, Mark Finlay, Ashley Price
Subject: Vegas, Baby!

So our event with Marsh 7 is this weekend in...VEGAS. YEAH! VEGAS BABY! I will be a pretty hip chick this weekend indeed. Everything for our event is done (hello, can you say organized!?) and so I'm really going to just capture it all on my phone. And, if I happen to snap a few photos of me with Marsh 7, so be it. I'm just excited to have an all-access pass to something...anything. For once, I'm gonna be cool. Hurrah! Okay, anyone who writes "Hurrah!" in an email cannot be THAT cool. But, nonetheless, this is close to cool as I'm ever gonna get.

From: Shelley Manning – July 29, 2011 – 4:02 PM
To: Mark Finlay, Ashley Price, Renee Greene
Subject: Re: Vegas, Baby!

Good luck, sweetie. I'm sure it will be an amazing event. And don't forget, you are SUPERMODEL RENEE!

From: Ashley Price – July 29, 2011 – 4:15 PM
To: Shelley Manning, Renee Greene; Mark Finlay
Subject: Re: Vegas, Baby!

Knock 'em dead!

From: Mark Finlay – July 29, 2011 – 5:30 PM
To: Shelley Manning, Ashley Price, Renee Greene
Subject: Re: Vegas, Baby!

"Hurrah" for Renee. (Guess I'm just not that cool either.)

From: Renee Greene – July 29, 2011 – 5:31 PM
To: Shelley Manning
Subject: Fwd: Re: Vegas, Baby!

Bite your tongue!

From: Shelley Manning – July 29, 2011 – 5:33 PM
To: Renee Greene
Subject: Fwd: Re: Vegas, Baby!

Fine. Anyway, I have a date tonight. Maybe he'll bite it for me. ;)

From: Renee Greene – July 31, 2011 – 10:07 PM
To: Shelley Manning, Mark Finlay, Ashley Price
Subject: 8th Grade Flashbacks :(

So, I am definitely not as cool as I thought after being at this event in Vegas. Now, considering I really didn't think I was all that cool to begin with, I've sunk to new lows. Let me start off by saying our event was great. The client was pleased and we had awesome consumer participation.

And, I must confess, the grass really is greener on the other side. Let's just say I felt really cool being on the inside of the barriers. No, I wasn't a lowly general consumer walking around and wondering if I would get a glimpse of someone who is a someone. I was being envied by other people. Now THAT hasn't happened in a really long time.
People were asking, begging, pleading to be let into the secure area where I was. And alas, they were rebuffed and sent away crying. (Okay, so they weren't crying. I'm adding a little dramatic license here. Just bear with me.)

But really, I felt like the most uncool person in the VIP area. In other words, I was the loser of the cool group. Can we say 8th grade all over again? UGH! The athletes looked at me (considering they never even spoke a word to me) as if I wasn't even there. Now granted, they were there for an exhibition and preparing to dazzle people with their extreme sports capabilities. Lord knows that if you really want to impress people, you've got to jump a BMX bike over a bunch of garbage cans. But still. They walked into an empty room and didn't even acknowledge that it wasn't really empty. I was there. However, it was cool to see Marsh 7. They only showed up for about 20 minutes. They were in a different secure location before their performance...ran to the green room after their set but before their encore. They were basically in their own little world except for Jason Kite, the bass player. He was so nice and asked me who I was and what I was doing there, how things were going, etc. He even asked for my card. Weird, huh?

From: Mark Finlay – July 31, 2011 – 10:26 PM
To: Renee Greene
Subject: Re: 8th Grade Flashbacks :(

So sorry to hear that Renee. As you well know, I think you're great.

From: Ashley Price – August 1, 2011 – 8:26 AM
To: Renee Greene
Subject: Re: 8th Grade Flashbacks :(

UGH! So sorry, Renee. It's hard to believe there are people out there who just feel superior to others. But, I don't really remember 8th grade being all that bad. We'll catch up properly with our lunch at Mel's.

From: Shelley Manning – August 1, 2011 – 9:53 AM
To: Renee Greene
Subject: Re: 8th Grade Flashbacks :(

How rude. You know, celebrities make me sick sometimes. Granted, I would love to be hanging out with them so I could look down on the little people. But since I'm a little person right now, they make me sick. They think they are so much better than everyone else. I'm sorry they were so rude to you. Little do they know that you are so worth knowing. But, that's pretty cool that Jason Kite was so chatty with you. Is he nice? Is he cute? DETAILS!!!

From: Renee Greene – August 1, 2011 – 11:07 AM
To: Shelley Manning
Subject: Re: 8th Grade Flashbacks :(

Actually, he was much cuter in person than I thought he would be. In the videos, he looks a bit greasy. He was quite grunge, but not in a dirty way. And he was much shorter than I expected, which made him all the more attractive. Like a real person and not some grandiose rock star. He was actually really nice. He seemed to be genuinely excited to be there and have the crowd so enthusiastic. I think he just felt sorry for me since everyone else was essentially ignoring me. And, they were actually really good live. Although they've never really been my style, they have some great songs.

From: Shelley Manning – August 1, 2011 – 11:15 AM
To: Renee Greene
Subject: Re: 8th Grade Flashbacks :(

Oooh. You know *I* like them dirty. ;)

From: Fly12271@easymailusa.com – August 4, 2011 – 11:02 AM
To: Renee Greene
Subject: Grab some dinner?

Hi Renee. It was great to meet you the other day. I'm going to be in LA in a few weeks and thought that maybe we could grab some dinner. Let me know if you are interested.

From: Renee Greene – August 4, 2011 – 11:07 AM
To: Shelley Manning
Subject: Fwd: Grab some dinner?

I have NO CLUE who this is from. He's not one of these Internet guys, because those all come via the service. And, I hid my profile for a while anyway. I'm racking my brains, but just can't think of who the heck this could be from. Thoughts?

From: Shelley Manning – August 4, 2011 – 11:17 AM
To: Renee Greene
Subject: Re: Fwd: Grab some dinner?

Hmmm. Think. Did you have any business meetings? Did you give your number out to anyone when we met for drinks at Flints last week? Nothing worse than an email from some random guy who wants to go out with you but you have no clue if he's a hottie or nottie or naughty (Ha! Ha!). Although, nothing better than finding out that some random guy who wants to go out with you IS a hottie. Dilemma? Yes. Solution? Yes. Just make plans. If worse comes to worse, you can always call Miss Priss and do the fake emergency thing again. That seemed to work well for you a few months ago.

From: Fly12271@easymailusa.com – August 4, 2011 – 12:15 PM
To: Renee Greene
Subject: Fwd: Grab some dinner?

Just realized that you probably have NO clue who that email was from. This is Jason Kite. We met at the MTV event in Vegas. Anyway, we're playing a few nights at the Roxy and I thought that you might be able to meet up for dinner at some point while I'm in town. Could also score tickets to the show for you if you want to come. Hope to hear from you.

From: Renee Greene – August 4, 2011 – 2:19 PM
To: Shelley Manning
Subject: Fwd: Fwd: Grab some dinner?

Okay. Am I just imaging things or is Jason Kite asking me on a date? A rock star wants to have dinner with me. Pinch me. I must be dreaming.

From: Shelley Manning – August 4, 2011 – 3:18 PM
To: Renee Greene
Subject: Re: Fwd: Fwd: Grab some dinner?

Holy crap! That is so awesome. And you thought he was just being nice to you out of pity. No, this man has good instincts and real smarts. He recognized right away that you were the quality among the quantity. Have dinner with him and get tickets for the show. Ask for backstage passes, too. The lead singer is a hottie and I want to meet him.

From: Renee Greene – August 4, 2011 – 4:47 PM
To: Fly12271@easymailusa.com
Subject: Re: Fwd: Grab some dinner?

Hi Jason. Thanks for the follow up email. I must confess, your email address did leave me racking my brain to figure out who exactly you were. Not that I give my info out to that many people. But, I just didn't expect to hear from you. I would love to meet up for dinner when you are in town. Are you sure you are going to have time? I'd think you'd be busy with sound checks, wardrobe checks, press interviews, etc. And, since you so kindly offered, I would love a few tickets to the show. My friend is really excited about seeing you guys in concert. Let me know what works for you.

From: Fly12271@easymailusa.com – August 4, 2011 – 7:18 PM
To: Renee Greene
Subject: Re: Fwd: Grab some dinner?

Sorry about that. I've got a real random email address so that I can have some anonymity when I'm ordering books online and other stuff like that. Yes, believe it or not, I read. ;) We are going to be pretty busy, but I would really like to make the time to see you. I really enjoyed talking with you at the MTV event. You seem really real. I know that must sound weird. But in this business, it's hard to meet people who are real. The other guys in the band are still really into this whole lifestyle, but I'm getting a bit tired of all of the phoniness and stuff. Wow! Didn't mean to get so deep on you. Anyway, I'll be coming into town on the 15th. Our shows are on the 17th and 18th. So, I could do dinner on the 16th or 19th and then if you want to come to the show either night, I'll get you and your friends backstage. Tell me how many tickets you need.

From: Renee Greene – August 4, 2011 – 8:27 PM
To: Fly12271@easymailusa.com
Subject: Re: Fwd: Grab some dinner?

I can understand the whole "real" thing, believe me. I bet it's hard to be living on the road and surrounded by people that probably want something from you. Dinner on the 16th sounds great. And, if I could get two tickets for the concert on the 17th, that would be great too. One for me and one for my friend.

From: Fly12271@easymailusa.com – August 4, 2011 – 9:36 PM
To: Renee Greene
Subject: Re: Fwd: Grab some dinner?

Two tickets, that's all? No problem. See, you are real. Most people hear "free tickets" and ask for like 20. I'll arrange for them to be at will call under your name. I'm really glad you are free for dinner. Why don't I give you a call at your office on Wednesday or Thursday and we can figure out the details. Sound good?

From: Renee Greene – August 4, 2011 – 9:39 PM
To: Fly12271@easymailusa.com
Subject: Re: Fwd: Grab some dinner?

That sounds great. I'll talk with you soon.

From: Renee Greene – August 5, 2011 – 9:16 AM
To: Shelley Manning
Subject: All Access

You are cordially invited to see Marsh 7 (BACKSTAGE!!!!) with me on Wednesday, August 17th. So, mark your calendar. Jason is going to have two tickets reserved for us at will call and I'm having dinner with him the night before. This is REALLY WEIRD.

From: Shelley Manning – August 5, 2011 – 10:31 AM
To: Renee Greene
Subject: Re: All Access

YAHOO! WOW! I am so excited. Did you tell him that I think the lead singer is totally hot and that I'm excited to meet him? I can't believe you are having dinner with him. Where are you guys going? Is he picking you up? in a limo? in a touring van? As always, DETAILS!!!

From: Renee Greene – August 5, 2011 – 2:57 PM
To: Shelley Manning
Subject: Re: All Access

No details to share yet. We haven't figured out all of that stuff. He's going to call me a few days before and we'll decide. I just wonder if he does this in every city. You know. Maybe he's tired of the groupies who are just there at his beck and call and wants a challenge. So, he picks some normal person and tries to woo them.

I'm also wondering if we have anything in common. I mean, I work for a PR firm. My clients make paint and cooking oil. What, if anything, will we have to talk about? He's a rock star for god sakes. And no, I did not tell him that you wanted to jump the lead singer. I thought that might be better conversation over dinner. ;)

From: Shelley Manning – August 5, 2011 – 4:07 PM
To: Renee Greene
Subject: Re: All Access

Yeah, explaining that I'm willing to do ANYTHING for the lead singer is probably good first-date conversation for you. But, more importantly, I highly doubt that he asked you out as some sort of game or quest. Did you ever, for once, consider the fact that he asked you out because you are smart and beautiful? No, that would likely never occur to you, my self confidence-challenged friend. If I have to remind you one more time that you have got to realize how incredible you are, I'm going to...well, I just don't know what I'm going to do. But, it won't be pretty. Trust me. Just try to go with it. And, when have you ever been at a loss for words. My god! You could talk the ear off of a deaf man on a hot summer day. Conversation will be the least of your worries.

From: Renee Greene – August 5, 2011 – 4:31 PM
To: Shelley Manning
Subject: Re: All Access

What should I be worried about, then? JUST KIDDING. You're right. Well, I gotta run, my groupie friend. I actually have REAL work to do. I'll talk with you tonight.

From: Renee Greene – August 8, 2011 – 11:13 AM
To: Shelley Manning, Ashley Price, Mark Finlay
Subject: Worst Nightmare Realized

Well, worst *career* nightmare. (Honestly, I think I've already lived through the worst dating nightmares possible!) So, I vowed that in my public relations career, I would never don a mascot costume. I never wanted to be the poor schlub roasting away in a hot mess of fur shaking hands with people at a mall or ballgame. And fortunately for me, during the early years of PR agency life in New York, I escaped mascot duty. I figured that as I moved up the corporate ladder, I would subject interns and other junior staff to this form of professional torture. But my worst nightmare has been realized. Our agency has prepared a game show for a client's sales meeting and one of the team members is sick. So, at the last minute, *MY* boss has dictated that I have to fly to Minneapolis (no, that's not the nightmare part, but it's close!) to play the role of Spamma White, game show hostess. Someone else will be portraying Pat Laidback, game show host. I need to wear an old bridesmaid's dress they found at a resale shop, smile incessantly and hand out Rice 'a Roni as consolation prizes to people who get the answers wrong.

From: Shelley Manning – August 8, 2011 – 11:17 AM
To: Renee Greene, Ashley Price, Mark Finlay
Subject: Re: Worst Nightmare Realized

I hear humiliation is the new black. You wear it well, you fashion goddess, you.

From: Ashley Price – August 8, 2011 – 12:05 PM
To: Renee Greene, Shelley Manning, Mark Finlay
Subject: Re: Worst Nightmare Realized

I think I'm going to pee in my pants from laughing. You MUST take photos.

From: Mark Finlay – August 8, 2011 – 12:11 PM
To: Renee Greene, Shelley Manning, Ashley Price
Subject: Re: Worst Nightmare Realized

I think that's kind of clever.

From: Renee Greene – August 8, 2011 – 1:15 PM
To: Shelley Manning, Ashley Price, Mark Finlay
Subject: Re: Worst Nightmare Realized

Mark, seriously? I know there are other indignities and injustices in the world that certainly trump this. But, I still think this form of public embarrassment is completely and utterly horrifying. Well, if this doesn't get me reincarnated in my next life as a tall, leggy blonde, I don't know WHAT will.

From: Renee Greene – August 11, 2011 – 9:27 PM
To: Shelley Manning
Subject: Public Humiliation – Part Deux

So, I thought dressing up like Spamma White would be the biggest humiliation of my lifetime. Well, it wasn't even the biggest humiliation of TODAY. We were up all last night rehearsing for the game show presentation. I slept for maybe two hours.

And since I don't drink coffee, I had no caffeine to keep me up. By the time the presentation rolled around, I was running on adrenaline and fumes. So, when I got on my flight home, I found three empty seats together, pulled up the arm rests, laid down and promptly fell asleep.

After a few hours, I woke up, stretched and went to use the ladies room. Every man on that flight was staring at me. I thought, can't a young professional woman take a flight for business without getting leers and stares from men. Really!

Well, I got to the bathroom to find the middle button on my blouse had popped open and my black lace bra was fully exposed for EVERYONE to see. Needless to say, I buttoned up and walked back to my seat with blinders on. I've never been more mortified in my entire life.

From: Shelley Manning – August 12, 2011 – 8:02 AM
To: Renee Greene
Subject: Re: Public Humiliation – Part Deux

Oh, sweetie. Visions of Cancun in college are dancing through my head. ;) Seriously, you don't know any of them and will never see them again. You should feel proud. Not that I'm into women, but you've got a great rack. So what if a few lonely businessmen got their jollies? They probably went home and paid a bit more attention to their sex-starved wives. You really were doing a public service. And, don't you have a date with a rock star in a week? I think he will appreciate a girl who knows how to flash.

Speaking of humiliation, I endured my own share the other night. I was caught – by the local police – "neked" in an apartment complex hot tub with a guy we will now refer to as Hot Head.

What is “neked” you might ask? Well, “naked” is having no clothes on. “Neked,” on the other hand, is having no clothes on and being up to no good. Let’s just say Hot Head was certainly “up” but I was really “good” until his neighbors called the cops. Hot Head got a little belligerent and ended up getting arrested. It was quite comical, really, albeit it a little embarrassing.

From: Renee Greene – August 12, 2011 – 8:10 AM
To: Shelley Manning
Subject: Re: Public Humiliation – Part Deux

LOL! I do feel a bit better. Thanks.

From: Renee Greene – August 14, 2011 – 9:11 AM
To: Shelley Manning, Ashley Price
Subject: How much does porn cost and can I expense it?

Well, I figured the subject line would certainly catch your attention. So, we have a client that flew into town for a few days to take part in a media training session and video shoot. I pay for his hotel on my corporate credit card and then expense it back to his company. I get the receipt from the hotel today and I see a charge for $16.95 for a movie. Does it really cost that much to watch a movie in your room? Or was he watching porn? How do I expense porn?

From: Ashley Price – August 14, 2011 – 9:15 AM
To: Renee Greene, Shelley Manning
Subject: Re: How much does porn cost and can I expense it?

YUCK! That’s just gross. I would talk to HR about that one.

From: Shelley Manning – August 14, 2011 – 9:43 AM
To: Renee Greene, Ashley Price
Subject: Re: How much does porn cost and can I expense it?

Definitely porn. Gotta hand it to him, the guy sure has balls. HA! HA!

From: Renee Greene – August 14, 2011 – 9:45 AM
To: Shelley Manning, Ashley Price
Subject: Re: How much does porn cost and can I expense it?

LOL!!!!!!

From: Renee Greene – August 17, 2011 – 10:12 AM
To: Shelley Manning
Subject: Tonight's the Night!

Hope you are psyched, jazzed, pumped, amped and overall totally stoked for the show tonight. I'll pick you up at 6:30.

From: Shelley Manning – August 17, 2011 – 10:13 AM
To: Renee Greene
Subject: Re: Tonight's the Night!

All of the above!!!!!

From: Renee Greene – August 18, 2011 – 9:05 AM
To: Fly12271@easymailusa.com
Subject: Thanks!

Jason: Thanks so much for dinner the other night. I had such a great time. I must confess, I was a bit skeptical about having dinner with you. I really didn't think we would have anything in common and sort of wondered why you would want to go out with a "normal" person. I mean, you've shown your refrigerator on "Cribs." But it was so much fun getting to know you. Thanks also for the tickets to the show. My friend and I had the BEST time.

From: Renee Greene – August 18, 2011 – 9:18 AM
To: Shelley Manning
Subject: Groupie Much?

I'm guessing you had a good time last night. Sorry to have interrupted while you and the drummer were getting, uh, um, "acquainted" – in what looked like a bit of a hard-core "cuddle," I might add – but I didn't want to leave without making sure you were okay.

Jason was so sweet. I told him I would give him a ride back to his hotel, so we got in the car, drove over and then just talked for about 4 hours, with the motor running. When I got up this morning (from my own house…get your mind out of the gutter, girl!) and went to turn on the engine, the battery was dead. UGH! I had to get a jump (again, mind out of the gutter!) so I could get to the office.

But it was all worth it. I'm just sorry that he is leaving tomorrow for Bakersfield. I think if he was a normal person, we could really have something. It was a fun little fling, and the man knows how to kiss.

But I know it could never be anything more. We talked about trying to date from a distance and both agreed that it would be really hard. After seeing what goes on backstage with all of the women (no offense to you, dear friend), I don't think I'm trusting enough to have a relationship like that.

From: Shelley Manning – August 18, 2011 – 11:07 AM
To: Renee Greene
Subject: Re: Groupie Much?

I had the BEST time last night. Steve is SO FRIGGIN HOT. I think I would cuddle for him! Wow! Did I just say that?!? What a great time. Thanks so much. When I saw the two of you leave together, I knew you wouldn't sleep with him. After that fiasco with Matt, I just knew you wouldn't jump in the sack with Jason. I, on the other hand, would and did and I'm not embarrassed to say so. So there! And, I must admit, your "had to get a jump" remark did cause a chuckle. You really know me too well. So, we've had our brushes with rock stars and can now go back to dating regular folk. At least it was fun while it lasted.

From: Renee Greene – August 18, 2011 – 12:01 PM
To: Shelley Manning
Subject: Re: Groupie Much?

Regular folk? Oh no. Not me. I've got a date tomorrow night with Zac Efron. Did I forget to mention that?

From: Shelley Manning – August 18, 2011 – 2:07 PM
To: Renee Greene
Subject: Re: Groupie Much?

Pretty boy Zac just doesn't do it for me. I need a real man, like Russell Crowe. You know, a beer-swilling, muscle-bulging, punch-throwing, manly man. Oh heck. Who I am kidding? I'd take Zac in a heartbeat too, just to say I did it. But seriously though, you don't need to sit alone at home just because you aren't dating a rock star. You need to get out there and start living. I know what a pisser it was when Matt turned out to be such a shit, and I know you really like this Jason guy. But I think you need to get back online and continue with the Internet dating thing.

From: Renee Greene – August 18, 2011 – 3:17 PM
To: Shelley Manning
Subject: Re: Groupie Much?

You like beer-swilling, muscle-bulging, punch-throwing, manly men? Really? I seem to recall someone known as "the Cuddler" lurking around your bedroom. He was more of a chardonnay-sipping, calculator-toting, guy. Don't you remember the marathon-mocking session we had at Mel's?

On another note, maybe you're right. I guess I'm never going to meet anyone just by sitting in my apartment and eating Chinese takeout. UGH! I don't know if I'm ready to go through all of this again, but I'll try. Call you tomorrow!

From: Fly12271@easymailusa.com – August 19, 2011 – 3:01 PM
To: Renee Greene
Subject: Re: Thanks!

Hey Renee. Just wanted to drop you a quick email before we head out for the next stop on the tour. Listen, our tour ends in a couple months. I know you didn't want to try this long distance thing. As much as I don't want to pressure you into a relationship, I think you are something special and don't want to miss out on anything that could be. So, think about it and I'll call you tomorrow.

From: Renee Greene – August 19, 2011 – 3:08 PM
To: Shelley Manning
Subject: Fwd: Re: Thanks!

So this is the message I got from Jason. He seems so sincere and so sweet. But, can he be trusted? My instincts say yes, but we all know where my instincts have gotten me. So no it is. We will just be friends. Although I'll look forward to his call tomorrow.

From: Shelley Manning – August 19, 2011 – 3:51 PM
To: Renee Greene
Subject: Re: Fwd: Re: Thanks!

Get that profile back on line, and toot sweet.

From: Renee Greene – August 19, 2011 – 4:07 PM
To: member.services@choosejews.com
Subject: My Profile

I was writing to request that you please place my profile back online. My ID# is 49628; Screen Name: PRGal1981.

From: member.services@choosejews.com – August 19, 2011 – 4:10 PM
To: Renee Greene
Subject: Re: My Profile

Profile has been reinstated.

CHAPTER 7 – BACK IN THE SADDLE AGAIN

From: meet@choosejews.com/GoBucs428 – August 24, 2011 – 9:56 AM
To: meet@choosejews.com/PRGal1981
Subject: Hi!

Hi PR Gal. You may remember me. My name's Ethan and I emailed you a while back. You told me about your theory on treadmills and LA walkers. Anyway, I know you mentioned that you were seeing someone. But, your profile is online, so I thought that maybe you were still open to meeting people. Anyway, if you are, check out my profile and maybe we can talk. Thanks.

From: meet@choosejews.com/PRGal1981 – August 24, 2011 – 10:07 AM
To: meet@choosejews.com/GoBucs428
Subject: Re: Hi!

WHAT THE HELL! This guy thinks that just because it's been a few months that I'm no longer seeing Matt. What, my profile and photo reek of "can't keep a relationship going"?!? What an ASS!

From: Renee Greene – August 24, 2011 – 10:08 AM
To: Shelley Manning
Subject: Fwd: Re: Hi!

SHIT! SHIT! SHIT! I thought I had forwarded this to you, but I hit reply by accident and sent this message to him. SHIT! SHIT! SHIT! What do I do?

From: Shelley Manning – August 24, 2011 – 10:11 AM
To: Renee Greene
Subject: Re: Fwd: Re: Hi!

Wow! I've seen you royally screw up before, but this takes the cake. HA-LARIOUS! I'm usually one for giving advice, but I have no guidance on this one. I'd LOVE to see his response, if any.

From: meet@choosejews.com/GoBucs428 – August 24, 2011 – 10:15 AM
To: meet@choosejews.com/PRGal1981
Subject: Re: Hi!

Okay then. Guess I can tell what you honestly think of me. Won't bother you anymore and good luck.

From: meet@choosejews.com/PRGal1981 – August 24, 2011 – 10:25 AM
To: meet@choosejews.com/GoBucs428
Subject: Re: Hi!

I am SO INCREDIBLY SORRY! That email was not meant for your eyes…obviously. My profile says nothing about being rude, and rightly so. I've just been going through some relationship stuff lately and was blowing off a little steam. Yikes! That makes me sound like a real ball buster, huh? That was meant for my best friend who usually gives great advice, keeps me grounded, and encourages me to meet new people. Again, my sincerest apologies. If you are still interested in meeting, why don't we try to have a drink? I promise I will come straight from an anger management self-help group, so I'll be nice and calm. (Just kidding).

From: meet@choosejews.com/GoBucs428 – August 24, 2011 – 11:17 AM
To: meet@choosejews.com/PRGal1981
Subject: Re: Hi!

Well, as long as you promise there will be no emotional or physical abuse, I'm game. Why don't we say the Coffee Shack on Beverly Glen…do you know where that is…on Saturday at noon?

From: meet@choosejews.com/PRGal1981 – August 24, 2011 – 11:36 AM
To: meet@choosejews.com/GoBucs428
Subject: Re: Hi!

I love the Coffee Shack. I don't drink coffee…never had a cup. I had a sip once and didn't like it so I never tried it again. Chocolate on the other hand…tried it, loved it and can't stop. ;) But Coffee Shack has these great vanilla blended drinks. It's like a really cold, rich glass of milk. YUM! Anyway, I digress. I live right down the street from the Coffee Shack and Saturday at noon sounds great. I'll be the one looking enormously apologetic.

From: meet@choosejews.com/GoBucs428 – August 24, 2011 – 11:42 AM
To: meet@choosejews.com/PRGal1981
Subject: Re: Hi!

Sounds great. I'm a fan of blendeds as well and I love regret in a woman. J/K. See you Saturday.

From: Renee Greene – August 24, 2011 – 12:15 PM
To: Shelley Manning
Subject: Fwd: Re: Hi!

Oh my. This guy seems pretty cool. He wrote back that he wouldn't bother me anymore after seeing my response and I apologized and explained that I'm certifiable, it wasn't meant for him, etc. Then we agreed to meet for a blended at the Coffee Shack. So I'm meeting him there on Saturday.

From: Shelley Manning – August 24, 2011 – 3:35 PM
To: Renee Greene
Subject: Re: Fwd: Re: Hi!

Wow! You really lead a charmed life. This will be a great story to tell your grandkids. Grandma completely insulted Grandpa in an email and called him an ass. But, he fell in love with her anyway. I love it!

From: Renee Greene – August 24, 2011 – 3:39 PM
To: Shelley Manning
Subject: Re: Fwd: Re: Hi!

This is weird. You're usually the one telling me not to jump ahead and wear my heart on my sleeve and *you've* got me married…with grandkids…to this guy. Has the world turned on its side? What's going on?

From: Shelley Manning – August 24, 2011 – 4:45 PM
To: Renee Greene
Subject: Re: Fwd: Re: Hi!

You're right. I'm becoming you and you're becoming me. All I can say is you are one lucky gal. Gotta run. Having drinks with a guy who from hence forth shall be known as the Trampoline. He likes to bounce me up and down. Now that's the kind of exercise I could get used to. Mwah! Mwah!

From: Renee Greene – August 27, 2011 – 2:27 PM
To: Shelley Manning
Subject: Cute or cut?

Well, Ethan is just about the cutest thing I've ever laid eyes on. He has beautiful blue eyes and is so sweet and smart. I could really see myself falling for him, which is why I'm tempted to never see him again. Please, talk me down from the ledge.

From: Shelley Manning – August 29, 2011 – 8:07 AM
To: Renee Greene
Subject: Re: Cute or cut?

Oh, Renee. Don't jump. No, don't jump. There, does that help? Oh puh-leaz. You know you want to see him again. You know you are going to see him again. Fine. If it makes you feel better…Renee, I don't want to hear any of this talk about not seeing a great guy again. You're just feeling scared and vulnerable. But as the old adage goes, better to have loved and lost than never loved at all. So go out with him again.

From: Renee Greene – August 29, 2011 – 8:15 AM
To: Shelley Manning
Subject: Re: Cute or cut?

Thanks. I feel much better. I know that was painful for you. I don't know how you put up with me.

From: Shelley Manning – August 29, 2011 – 8:22 AM
To: Renee Greene
Subject: Re: Cute or cut?

Me neither, sweetie. Just kidding. I put up with you because we've been friends for so long and you have too much dirt on me.

From: Renee Greene – August 29, 2011 – 8:23 AM
To: Shelley Manning
Subject: Re: Cute or cut?

Thanks. :)

From: meet@choosejews.com/GoBucs428 – August 29, 2011 – 9:53 AM
To: meet@choosejews.com/PRGal1981
Subject: Re: Hi!

Just wanted to drop you an email and say thanks for the blended on Saturday. It was really nice getting to know you. Was wondering if you were free for dinner this weekend. My schedule is pretty open, so let me know if you are interested/available. Oh, and my regular email address is PBCupLover@easymailusa.com.

From: Renee Greene – August 29, 2011 – 10:13 AM
To: PBCupLover@easymailusa.com
Subject: Dinner Plans

I would love to have dinner this weekend. I've got plans on Friday, but could do it on Saturday night. Let me know what time works for you and if you want to meet there or pick me up. Looking forward to it.

From: PBCupLover@easymailusa.com – August 29, 2011 – 2:36 PM
To: Renee Greene
Subject: Re: Dinner Plans

Why don't I come pick you up? Let's make this a proper date.

From: Renee Greene – August 29, 2011 – 2:52 PM
To: PBCupLover@easymailusa.com
Subject: Re: Dinner Plans

Sounds good to me. I'm at the southwest corner of Pico and Beverly Glen, #402.

CHAPTER 8: A NORMAL, HEALTHY RELATIONSHIP?

From: Renee Greene – September 4, 2011 – 7:02 AM
To: PBCupLover@easymailusa.com
Subject: Great Time

Good morning. Didn't want to call this early but before I head out for the day, I wanted to say thank you for a great night last night. I had a wonderful time. Looking forward to seeing you later in the week.

From: Renee Greene – September 4, 2011 – 7:15 AM
To: Shelley Manning
Subject: What a night!

Didn't want to call you too early in the morning, especially after a Saturday night. For all I know, your hot date with some guy who will from now on be referred to as some hilarious nickname are still engaged in whatever scandalous activities that typically make me VERY jealous.

But, I'm just beaming after my second date with Ethan. He is AWESOME. I don't want to jinx things, but I really feel a special connection here. We had dinner at a little Japanese place in Santa Monica and then just walked around Third Street and Montana for a while. We just talked and talked and talked. He is so interesting and has a real corny sense of humor, which I totally dig. And we sat on a little bench and kissed for a while. It was really sweet.

I told him that I have been burned before by jumping into things too fast. He said he totally understood and would let me set the pace for our relationship.

All in all, a great start to what I think could be something serious.

From: PBCupLover@easymailusa.com – September 4 – 10:16 AM
To: Renee Greene
Subject: Re: Great Time

I had a great time too. Gotta say, your Choose Jews profile was spot on. I like that. I'll give you a call later today or tomorrow and we can figure out some plans for later this week. Have a great day.

From: Shelley Manning – September 5, 2011 – 9:07AM
To: Renee Greene
Subject: Re: What a night!

Well, you do know me well. I was tied up all weekend (literally!) by a guy who will be known as Boy Scout because he knew all sorts of interesting knots. But sounds like you have nothing to be jealous about. Seems like you've got a real winner there. I'll look forward to meeting him/mocking him/judging him, etc. ;) Mwah! Mwah!

From: meet@choosejews.com/SMacher25 – September 6, 2011 – 10:32 AM
To: meet@choosejews.com/PRGal1981
Subject: Hello

Hi my name is Shlomo, but don't let that scare you off. I was raised an Orthodox Jew but started to question my faith a few years back and have scaled back to be a happy Conservative.

The Orthodox culture was a bit too stringent for me. Plus, I started a love affair with bacon. ;) Anyway, I was hoping you would take a look at my profile and we could talk. Thanks for your time.

From: meet@choosejews.com/ PRGal1981 – September 6, 2011 – 11:05 AM
To: meet@choosejews.com/ SMacher25
Subject: Re: Hello

Hi Shlomo. Thanks so much for your email. I hear you on the bacon. I have a dear friend who's personal mantra is "Everything tastes better wrapped in bacon." You seem like a really nice guy, but I've recently met someone through Choose Jews and I've been remiss about not hiding my profile. Best of luck in finding the right girl for you. I'm sure there's a bacon lover out there just waiting for ya.

From: meet@choosejews.com/SMacher25 – September 6, 2011 – 11:12 AM
To: meet@choosejews.com/PRGal1981
Subject: Re: Hello

Thanks for your note back PR Gal. Most people would have just ignored my message. But you took the time to read it and respond. That's really nice. If things don't work out with this guy, please keep me in mind. Thanks for your time.

From: PBCupLover@easymailusa.com – September 12, 2011 – 8:54 AM
To: Renee Greene
Subject: Continued Discussion

Okay, so to continue our discussion from last night, which was a great time by the way, I just don't get it. It's a complete mystery to me. Probably the biggest mystery beyond how the Egyptian's built the Pyramids. How you could have/need/want so many pairs of shoes? Please, I beg of you, please explain!!!!

From: Renee Greene – September 12, 2011 – 9:42 AM
To: PBCupLover@easymailusa.com
Subject: Re: Continued Discussion

It's just a girl thing. I think part of it has to do with women having low self-esteem. We may not like the way our clothes fit and always be thinking we could lose some weight here or there, but our shoes ALWAYS fit.

I think the biggest mystery of our time is a bit more modern… and musical. Bear with me on this. Meatloaf sings, "I would do anything for love, but I won't do that." And, Hall & Oats sing "I can't go for that. No can do." What is *that* which these man cannot do? Tell me, please, oh wise one.

From: PBCupLover@easymailusa.com – September 12, 2011 – 8:01 PM
To: Renee Greene
Subject: Re: Continued Discussion

I'm stumped. I've been racking my brains all day – in between work, of course – to come up with something clever to say back. But, I'm truly stumped. Let's just say there is nothing I wouldn't do for you.

From: Renee Greene – September 13, 2011 – 8:22 AM
To: PBCupLover@easymailusa.com
Subject: Re: Continued Discussion

<blush>

From: Shelley Manning – September 13, 2011 – 10:28 AM
To: Renee Greene
Subject: I'M ENGAGED…

…in a lot of work projects right now and don't think I can make it to lunch at Mel's. The evil corporate trolls are on a rampage. Rain check?

From: Renee Greene – September 13, 2011 – 10:29 AM
To: Shelley Manning
Subject: Re: I'M ENGAGED…

OMG! When I saw the subject of your email, I just about fell out of my chair. Don't scare me like that. Yes, rain check.

From: Shelley Manning – September 14, 2011 – 11:07 AM
To: Renee Greene
Subject: I'M PREGNANT…

…with ideas for making it look like I'm busy at work, when in fact, I'm attending to personal matters.

From: Renee Greene – September 14, 2011 – 11:09 AM
To: Shelley Manning
Subject: Re: I'M PREGNANT…

OMG AGAIN! You have to stop that. I get a pop up in the middle of my computer screen showing me the sender and subject of emails as they arrive. Behave!

From: Shelley Manning – September 15, 2011 – 8:21 AM
To: Renee Greene
Subject: I'M MARRIED…

…to my job right now. We are so darn busy and the corporate trolls are cracking down.

From: Shelley Manning – September 15, 2011 – 9:32 AM
To: Renee Greene
Subject: Re: I'M MARRIED…

Stop it. STOP IT. STOP IT!

---

enee Greene – September 17, 2011 – 2:58 PM
ley Manning, Mark Finlay, Ashley Price
Disney Horror Show

Ugh! I have the WORST cold. I'm Sneezy, Sleepy and Grumpy all rolled into one. Rain check on Flint's for me. Have fun!

From: Mark Finlay – September 17, 2011 – 3:15 PM
To: Shelley Manning, Renee Greene, Ashley Price
Subject: Re: Disney Horror Show

Feel better!

From: Ashley Price – September 17, 2011 – 4:00 PM
To: Shelley Manning, Mark Finlay, Renee Greene
Subject: Re: Disney Horror Show

Let me know if you need anything and get better soon.

From: Shelley Manning – September 17, 2011 – 4:05 PM
To: Renee Greene, Mark Finlay, Ashley Price
Subject: Re: Disney Horror Show

I like it better when you're Happy and Bashful – you know, your normal self. Feel better!

From: Renee Greene – September 18, 2011 – 1:30 PM
To: Shelley Manning, Mark Finlay, Ashley Price
Subject: Cloud Nine!!!!!

Dank you berry much. Translation: Thank you very much. That's what I said to my wonderful "boyfriend" (yes, you read correctly – boyfriend!!!) who just dropped off matzo ball soup from Marty's upon hearing that I have the WORST cold in the history of colds.

He knocked on the door and said he didn't want to disturb me but thought I could use some Jewish penicillin. When I said "Dank you berry much" he responded, "Well of course. That's what boyfriends do when their girlfriends are sick." I almost melted. Really, I sneezed. But, I almost melted. Despite the non-stop snot drip, pounding headache, mild fever and hacking cough, I've never felt better. Hurrah!

From: Shelley Manning – September 18, 2011 – 1:38 PM
To: Ashley Price, Mark Finlay, Renee Greene
Subject: Re: Cloud Nine!!!!!

You so deserve that, sweetie. Not the cold. But, the thoughtful boyfriend. Yeah!

From: Mark Finlay – September 18, 2011 – 2:02 PM
To: Shelley Manning, Ashley Price, Renee Greene
Subject: Re: Cloud Nine!!!!!

AW! That is so sweet. Enjoy all of the happiness and attention.

From: Ashley Price – September 18, 2011 – 4:45 PM
To: Shelley Manning, Mark Finlay, Renee Greene
Subject: Re: Cloud Nine!!!!!

That's the sign of a great boyfriend. Not that I would know. Evan has been a complete loser lately. I'm thinking it's over for good this time. But, I'm happy for you. Just don't get your hopes up too high. He might turn out to be a real jerk in the end.

From: Shelley Manning – September 18, 2011 – 4:48 PM
To: Renee Greene
Subject: Fwd: Re: Cloud Nine!!!!!

UGH! How do you put up with her? You listen to me. Keep those hopes up as high as you want. He sounds like a keeper.

From: Renee Greene – September 18, 2011 – 8:02 PM
To: Shelley Manning
Subject: Re: Fwd: Re: Cloud Nine!!!!!

Dank you berry much! <cough, cough>

From: Renee Greene – September 18, 2011 – 8:05 PM
To: PBCupLover@easymailusa.com
Subject: Jewish Penicillin Indeed!

Thank you! Thank you! I can't believe you ventured over here – without a hazmat suit on – just to bring me soup. You are such a sweetheart!

From: PBCupLover@easymailusa.com – September 18, 2011 – 9:12 PM
To: Renee Greene
Subject: Re: Jewish Penicillin Indeed!

Of course. You feel better soon! I just arrived in San Francisco. I'll call you in the morning to check in on you.

From: meet@choosejews.com/CrimsonGuy30 – September 21, 2011 – 11:04 AM
To: meet@choosejews.com/PRGal1981
Subject: New Lady?

Hello! My name is Dylan and I'm new to Los Angeles and Choose Jews. I just moved here from Boston where I was getting my PhD in English Literature at Harvard. I just started a faculty position at Loyola. I figured with a new job and new city, there might be a new lady out there for me. I thought your profile smacked of someone truly genuine. I would love to get to know you better. Hoping to hear back from you.

From: meet@choosejews.com/ PRGal1981 – September 21, 2011 – 11:20 AM
To: meet@choosejews.com/CrimsonGuy30
Subject: Re: New Lady?

Thanks for your note Dylan. Wow! Harvard. Impressive. You sound like a very interesting (and smart) man. And the fact that you read is a huge plus. Hard to believe there are people in this day and age that don't read for pleasure.

But, I've recently met someone through the site and am hoping to see where that leads. I should have removed my profile, but just have forgotten to do so. Hope you do find that "new lady" you are looking for. Good luck.

From: Renee Greene – September 21, 2011 – 11:22 AM
To: member.services@choosejews.com
Subject: Profile on Hold

I was writing to request that you please hide my profile from viewing until further notice. My ID# is 49628; Screen Name: PRGal1981.

From: member.services@choosejews.com – September 21, 2011 – 11:24 AM
To: Renee Greene
Subject: Re: Profile on Hold

Profile has been hidden until further request.

From: Shelley Manning – September 22, 2011 – 7:53 AM
To: Renee Greene
Subject: LMAO…Great Story You'll LOVE

Okay, so I'm in SF at an industry conference this week doing some scouting and recruiting – for the company of course. I would never, EVER take this meeting of highly intelligent, successful and wealthy financial specimens as an opportunity to benefit personally. ;)

So, I meet this competing recruiter named Todd. We slip out of the conference and he slips into me. Then, right after he comes, he starts crying. LMAO! From now on, he will be referred to as The Toddler. Speaking of which, bumped into the Cuddler. Thought you would want to know, seeing as you are such a fan. Apparently, he's met a wonderful girl and is really happy.

From: Renee Greene – September 22, 2011 – 9:07 AM
To: Shelley Manning
Subject: Re: LMAO...Great Story You'll LOVE

The Toddler and the Cuddler in the same room. I thought you dealt with titans of the financial world, not wimpy little girly men. And, the Cuddler is seeing someone. I wonder who is the woman in THAT relationship?!?

From: Shelley Manning – September 22, 2011 – 9:10 AM
To: Renee Greene
Subject: Re: LMAO...Great Story You'll LOVE

So glad I told you, sweetie. I knew you would love this story. And, I certainly love seeing the she-devil in you come out.

From: Renee Greene – September 23, 2011 – 10:24 AM
To: Shelley Manning
Subject: Pure Exhaustion!

I'm spent. <u>Emotionally</u> spent. (Please, focus here.) Ethan <u>slept</u> over last night. (Again, focus!) and when I woke up, he was gone. No trace of him. Of course, I'm thinking this is a Matt situation all over again. Love 'em and leave 'em but this time without the sex.

So as I'm roaming around my apartment with tears streaming down my face, because apparently just the sight of me sleeping (fully clothed, mind you) with traces of drool seeping from my mouth is enough to send this guy running. All of the sudden, my buzzer starts buzzing. It's Ethan. He's downstairs. He slipped out to get a coffee because he knew I wouldn't have any at my apartment. And he brought me a vanilla blended and a chocolate croissant from Coffee Shack. He realized as he was halfway back that he didn't take my key to let himself back in. He kept apologizing for screwing up what he was hoping would be a very romantic gesture. UGH! The roller coaster that is dating!

From: Shelley Manning – September 24, 2011 – 8:22 AM
To: Renee Greene
Subject: Re: Pure Exhaustion!

I was on a dating roller coaster myself. But, this was one of those incredibly fun rides with a guy named Franklin. He will now, from this point forward, be referred to as the Cyclone. Topsy, turvy fun!

From: Renee Greene – September 26, 2011 – 10:55 AM
To: PBCupLover@easymailusa.com
Subject: Happy "Month-Aversary"

Hi there. About to get on a call with a client and the Wall Street Journal. And I'm so nervous. Crazy, huh? I won't even be saying a word – just sitting on the phone while the client talks and taking notes. Nonetheless, I'm a bundle of nerves.

Another thing I forgot to put in my Choose Jews profile. I'm slightly – only slightly, neurotic. I know. False advertising. We in PR just like to call it message control.

Anyway, wanted to say happy Month-Aversary and let you know how lucky I feel that I met you one month ago today. Hope you are having a great day and I'll call you tonight.

From: PBCupLover@easymailusa.com – September 26, 2011 – 10:59 AM
To: Renee Greene
Subject: Re: Happy "Month-Aversary"

What a great surprise. I'm the lucky one. In the middle of a meeting and getting glaring looks for typing on my phone. Call you later.

From: Mark Finlay – September 29, 2011 – 10:56 PM
To: Renee Greene
Subject: It's a Man, Baby!

Sorry I have been incommunicado for a while. Working like a mad man on the game sequel. But, wanted to tell you a hilarious story. So, I get a dating service email from…a guy! To quote a great Seinfeld episode, "Not that there's anything wrong with that," but I'm not gay. And, I'm pretty sure my profile says I'm only interested in women. But, rather than delete it, I decide to see what it says. It's actually from a woman using her guy friend's email account because she doesn't have one set up of her own yet. She's a psychologist who just moved here from Portland. I emailed her back, we've been talking for a week, and she seems really great. I know how incredibly happy you are with Ethan and I thought you would like to know that I too am finding success with online dating – finally! I'm hoping to meet her for dinner next week.

From: Renee Greene – September 30, 2011 – 9:18 AM
To: Mark Finlay
Subject: Re: It's a Man, Baby!

OMG! I'm SO SORRY to burst your bubble, but this chick did the SAME THING to Ethan. He told me a story about a psychologist who just moved here from out of town and contacted him using her friend's account. He went out for dinner with her and he said she's a total psycho. I'm SO, SO, SO SORRY. But, I figured you'd want to know sooner rather than later.

From: Mark Finlay – September 30, 2011 – 9:58 AM
To: Renee Greene
Subject: Re: It's a Man, Baby!

Wow! Thanks for the warning. That sure is disappointing. But you're right. Better to find out now. So, what do I do? Just not email her back? Call her out on it?

From: Renee Greene – September 30, 2011 – 10:12 AM
To: Mark Finlay
Subject: Re: It's a Man, Baby!

Well, you know me. I'm the queen of non-confrontation. However, from experience, let me tell you, it's so much easier to tell someone off online versus in person. So, if you feel comfortable, tell her that you know she's pulled this stunt with other guys and you're just not interested in her drama and lies. Ooooh., that sounds pretty good. See what I mean?

From: Mark Finlay – September 30, 2011 – 10:18 AM
To: Renee Greene
Subject: Re: It's a Man, Baby!

That does sound good. But I'm not sure I'm there yet. And knowing that she's done this before, and recalling our conversations about her psychology research, I'm wondering if I'm just part of a big experiment. I think I just won't email her back.

From: Mark Finlay – October 1, 2011 – 9:56 PM
To: Renee Greene
Subject: Fwd: Is everything okay?

Renee: See below from the psycho psychologist. I guess I've really pushed her buttons. I think the tables have turned. The psychology lab rat has become the psychology master. This is the third email she's sent in three days.

Mark: Is everything okay? I've tried now several times to reach you. I thought we were getting along so well. Did I do or say something to offend you?

From: Renee Greene – October 2, 2011 – 8:12 AM
To: Mark Finlay
Subject: Re: Fwd: Is everything okay?

Hilarious. I told Ethan all about it. He (adorable thing he is) blushed and felt a little embarrassed that he didn't see through the sham. He says you're his new hero and he looks forward to meeting you soon.

From: Renee Greene – October 3, 2011 – 9:17 AM
To: PBCupLover@easymailusa.com
Subject: Photo

Came out pretty good, huh?

From: PBCupLover@easymailusa.com – October 3, 2011 – 10:50 AM
To: Renee Greene
Subject: Re: Photo

Wow. That picture came out great. I already forwarded it to my folks and my best friend Jason and printed it out on a color printer at work to show you off.

From: Renee Greene – October 3, 2011 – 11:02 AM
To: PBCupLover@easymailusa.com
Subject: Re: Photo

Oh my! I had no idea that by emailing you the picture, I was triggering a forwarding spree across America and that it would be printed out for your entire office to see. Yikes! Next time, "Supermodel Renee" is going to need to get permission from her agent to send a photo out that can easily be duplicated. I can just see these pictures ending up in the National Enquirer or Star Magazine. The paparazzi follow me around incessantly, you know.

From: PBCupLover@easymailusa.com – October 3, 2011 – 11:05 AM
To: Renee Greene
Subject: Re: Photo

Supermodel Renee, huh?

From: Renee Greene – October 3, 2011 – 11:20 AM
To: PBCupLover@easymailusa.com
Subject: Re: Photo

Oh yes, Supermodel Renee. I know what you're thinking. My girlfriend is a supermodel. SCORE! Well, let me explain: So, one time in college I was out at a bar and this guy comes over to me and says, "Hi. Who's your friend?" That happened a lot with my best friend. She's one of those really confident, hot chicks that guys fall over themselves to meet.

Anyway, I started talking with the guy and told him my name was Renee. A minute later he asked, "What's your name again? Sorry. I forgot. I'm just really bad with names." I said, "It's Renee. Next time you see me just think of something that reminds you of me and of my name. For example, see that guy over there? He's a total tool. His last name is Hammer. So, whenever I see him, I remember what a tool he is and then I remember he's Marcus Hammer. So, next time you see me, just think Supermodel and Renee – Supermodel Renee." He laughed. I told him I wasn't trying to be funny and he laughed again. But, he never forgot my name. And from then forward, I was known in college as Supermodel Renee.

From: PBCupLover@easymailusa.com – October 3, 2011 – 11:25 AM
To: Renee Greene
Subject: Re: Photo

You are a supermodel in my book.

From: Renee Greene – October 3, 2011 – 11:26 AM
To: PBCupLover@easymailusa.com
Subject: Re: Photo

<blush>

From: Renee Greene – October 5, 2011 – 9:02 AM
To: Shelley Manning, Ashley Price
Subject: Sorry!!!

Sorry I've been so out of the loop and haven't called either of you back. Ethan and I have either been together every night or on the phone into the early mornings.

I fear that I'm become what I've *always* despised: the girl who gives her best pals the shaft when a new guy comes into her life. My sincerest apologies!

Can I make it up to you with lunch – on me! – at Mel's tomorrow? I promise not to monopolize the conversation with my bliss.

From: Shelley Manning– October 5, 2011 – 10:43 AM
To: Renee Greene, Ashley Price
Subject: Re: Sorry!!!

No worries, sweetie. There's not much you could do, that I couldn't forgive. And if anyone deserves the bliss, it's you. Lunch tomorrow doesn't work for me, though. How about Friday?

From: Ashley Price– October 5, 2011 – 12:23 PM
To: Renee Greene, Shelley Manning
Subject: Re: Sorry!!!

As I was reading Shelley's response, I thought it was going to say, "If anyone deserves the shaft, it's Ashley." Friday lunch works for me. See you then.

From: Shelley Manning– October 5, 2011 – 1:12 PM
To: Renee Greene, Ashley Price
Subject: Re: Sorry!!!

HA-LARIOUS! While I may have been thinking that, I wouldn't have put it in writing, Ashley. ;)

From: Ashley Price– October 5, 2011 – 1:14 PM
To: Renee Greene, Shelley Manning
Subject: Re: Sorry!!!

Actually, I wouldn't put it past you. ;)

From: Renee Greene – October 5, 2011 – 2:34 PM
To: Shelley Manning, Ashley Price
Subject: Re: Sorry!!!

Perfect! I will see you both on Friday.

From: Renee Greene – October 5, 2011 – 2:35 PM
To: Shelley Manning
Subject: Fwd: Re: Sorry!!!

My, my. You and Ashley seem to be having a nice little rapport going. Me thinks me smells a friendship blooming.

From: Shelley Manning– October 5, 2011 – 9:02 AM
To: Renee Greene
Subject: Re: Fwd: Re: Sorry!!!

Okay, you know how I just said there's not much you could do that I wouldn't forgive. You're bordering. See you Fri.

From: PBCupLover@easymailusa.com – October 9, 2011 – 6:02 AM
To: Renee Greene
Subject: Big Apple Bound

Hey there. Have a terrific trip to New York – including a safe flight, my little fraidy cat – and I'll see you at the airport when you get back.

From: Renee Greene – October 9, 2011 – 6:05 AM
To: PBCupLover@easymailusa.com
Subject: Re: Big Apple Bound

:) !!!!!!!

From: PBCupLover@easymailusa.com – October 13, 2011 – 8:00 PM
To: Renee Greene
Subject: Tomorrow Night!

Looking forward to a romantic night with you tomorrow night. I'll pick you up at the airport at 6:15.

From: Renee Greene – October 13, 2011 – 11:52 PM
To: PBCupLover@easymailusa.com
Subject: Re: Tomorrow Night

I was hoping for a little less romance and a little more, you know.

From: Renee Greene – October 14, 2011 – 11:53 PM
To: Shelley Manning
Subject: Fwd: Re: Tomorrow Night

Yikes! I meant to hit "delete" not "send." What have I gotten myself into? What do I write back? Looking for your sage advice.

From: PBCupLover@easymailusa.com – October 14, 2011 – 9:02 AM
To: Renee Greene
Subject: Re: Tomorrow Night

REALLY!?!? "You know?" I don't. Why don't you tell me? ;) And don't be stingy with the details.

From: Shelley Manning – October 14, 2011 – 10:57 AM
To: Renee Greene
Subject: Re: Fwd: Re: Tomorrow Night

HA-LARIOUS! Modern technology can be a real kicker sometimes, huh?

Well, if you're looking for some dirty talk, you've come to the right place. But you clearly already knew that. ;) Why don't you send him an X-rated fill in the blank.

From: Renee Greene – October 14, 2011 – 11:07 AM
To: Shelley Manning
Subject: Re: Fwd: Re: Tomorrow Night

Wha?!?!

From: Shelley Manning – October 14, 2011 – 12:30 PM
To: Renee Greene
Subject: Re: Fwd: Re: Tomorrow Night

You know – a fill in the blank. A little story with fill in the blank verbs, adjectives, objects, etc. For example, I want to <insert verb> your <insert adjective> <insert noun> until the sun comes up.

From: Renee Greene – October 14, 2011 – 12:37 PM
To: Shelley Manning
Subject: Re: Fwd: Re: Tomorrow Night

OMG! I'm not sure I can do that!

From: Shelley Manning – October 14, 2011 – 12:39 PM
To: Renee Greene
Subject: Re: Fwd: Re: Tomorrow Night

Sure you can. Just use your imagination. Go for it. I guarantee he will LOVE it. And feel free to bcc me if you want.

From: Renee Greene – October 14, 2011 – 12:40 PM
To: Shelley Manning
Subject: Re: Fwd: Re: Tomorrow Night

No "bcc" here.

From: Shelley Manning – October 14, 2011 – 12:41 PM
To: Renee Greene
Subject: Re: Fwd: Re: Tomorrow Night

Darn!

From: Renee Greene – October 14, 2011 – 1:30 PM
To: PBCupLover@easymailusa.com
Subject: Re: Tomorrow Night

Fill in the blanks…

When I get back, I can't wait to put my <insert body part> on your <insert body part> and <insert verb> like there's no tomorrow. After I < insert verb> your < insert adjective> <insert body part> you are going to be so <insert adjective>, you'll be begging me for mercy. And just when you think you can't take anymore, we'll <insert verb> until the sun comes up. :)

From: PBCupLover@easymailusa.com – October 14, 2011 – 1:35 PM
To: Renee Greene
Subject: Re: Tomorrow Night

ZING! I'm in an inter-company meeting right now. Thank god I'm sitting at the conference table. Where is a cold shower when I need one? See you in a few hours.

p.s. I'm going to <verb> your <body part> for <length of time>!

From: Renee Greene – October 14, 2011 – 1:38 PM
To: PBCupLover@easymailusa.com
Subject: Re: Tomorrow Night

ZING!

From: Renee Greene – October 14, 2011 – 4:07 PM
To: Shelley Manning
Subject: EW!

Thank GOD for inflight WiFi!

The CREEPIEST thing just happened to me. So I'm exhausted, absolutely exhausted from a week of trade show madness. Ethan is picking me up from the airport tonight and after the racy fill-in-the-blank I sent him, (Thanks by the way. I channeled my inner Shelley and it was an erotic masterpiece, if I do say so myself!) I know tonight is going to be THE night.

I get on the plane and sit in my usual aisle seat as close to an exit as possible. Yes, I know. I'm paranoid and crazy. Flying is the safest mode of transportation, blah, blah, blah. It's an irrational fear, but I've embraced it wholeheartedly. But I digress. There is no one in my row, so I tilt my seat back, stuff my pillow onto the seat next to me and promptly fall asleep.

Apparently, we take off from LaGuardia, land in Philly, take off from Philly and I'm still sound asleep. I slowly awake, yawn and stretch to find a strange little man sitting next to me in the window seat. Apparently, unbeknownst to me, he boarded in Philly and CRAWLED over me into his seat.

He is leaning over the middle seat staring at me. And in a squeaky, high pitched voice says, "You've been asleep for a loooonnnng time." I reply, "Why, yes, I have." And he says, "You have really long eyelashes." EW! I explained that I have a tremendous amount of work I need to do prior to landing in LA and have buried myself in my laptop click clacking away furiously to you. EW! EW! EW!

But, thoughts of Ethan are dancing in my head and I can't wait for tonight. There is something truly special about this guy. I've never felt this way. Not even with Derrick.

From: Shelley Manning – October 14, 2011 – 4:22 PM
To: Renee Greene
Subject: Re: Ew!

Oh sweetie. I'm so happy for you. Not happy that some squeaky little man was getting his jollies watching your eyelashes flutter up and down as you slept. But happy that you are so content in this relationship. Now let's just hope the chemistry in the bedroom lives up to expectations. Can't wait to hear the details. Safe travels, sweetie! Mwah! Mwah!

From: Renee Greene – October 14, 2011 – 5:53 PM
To: Shelley Manning
Subject: Re: EW!

Thanks. I've been asked to shut down since we are preparing for landing. My little squeaky friend is giddy with excitement, as he realizes I'll be a captive audience for the next 25 minutes. Lord help me!

From: Shelley Manning – October 16, 2011 – 9:53 AM
To: Renee Greene
Subject: DETAILS, PLEASE

Welcome home. How was the trade show? How was your homecoming, or should I say homeCOMING? If it was anything like my homecoming from El Camino High, you had a FANTASTIC night. ;)

From: Renee Greene – October 16, 2011 – 10:02 AM
To: Shelley Manning
Subject: Re: DETAILS, PLEASE

I'm telling you, we pretty much jumped each other the moment we opened the door. It lasted for less than five minutes! I felt like I had been punched in the gut. Finally, I meet the man of my dreams and he just can't keep it going. He was totally embarrassed and said that I had just gotten him so turned on with my risqué mad lib – and the fact that we waited so long to finally do it – he just couldn't help but explode. We waited about a half hour, did it again, and it was WONDERFUL. He's WONDERFUL. Life is WONDERFUL.

As we lay in bed together, we started talking about all sorts of things and then had "the talk." Very interesting. I told him about all of my sexual conquests – all 4 of them including Surfer Dave from the dorm who I slept with on the first night of college just to lose my virginity. I also told him about Derrick. Don't worry. I didn't go into horrible details like I do with you. I just explained that I thought we were in love and on our three-year anniversary instead of proposing, he told me that he didn't see marriage in our future and it was probably better to end things.

He confided that he's been with 9 women and had two serious relationships as follows:

- Sex with two girls in high school – one the night of the prom. Two flings in college including a one night stand after a sorority formal.
- One serious girlfriend in college that ended when they both went off to grad school. She's now a married dermatology resident in Brooklyn and they are still friends.
- A short-lived relationship with a performance artist in the village, which he says still gives him nightmares.

- One serious relationship with a woman named Katarina that he used to work with. He thought she could be the one and then he found out she was cheating on him. So, he got a job transfer to the LA branch, but still had to deal with her. So, he quit and found another job.
- A little fling in LA with some chick he met at work. But, he knew they just weren't right for each other and didn't want to make the same mistake of being involved with someone at work and have it turn out badly.
- And me!

Actually, not a bad little run for him, huh?

From: Shelley Manning – October 16, 2011 – 12:05 PM
To: Renee Greene
Subject: Re: DETAILS, PLEASE

Very respectable numbers…for an amateur. Ha! Just kidding. So glad things are going well. So, when do I get to meet him/judge him/mock him?

From: Renee Greene – October 16, 2011 – 12:06 PM
To: Shelley Manning
Subject: Re: DETAILS, PLEASE

Soon enough, my friend. Soon enough.

From: Fly12271@easymailusa.com – October 16, 2011 – 12:10 PM
To: Renee Greene
Subject: Long time, no talk

Hi Renee. Hope you are doing well. We just wrapped up our tour and I'm heading to LA for a while. I know last time we spoke, you decided it would be best to just be "friends." And I totally get it. But, I also don't give up that easily. Maybe we could have dinner and talk. I hope to hear from you soon.

From: Renee Greene – October 16, 2011 – 1:45 PM
To: Fly12271@easymailusa.com
Subject: Re: Long time, no talk

Jason, so great to hear from you. Congrats on finishing the tour. I imagine you are exhausted. So, what opportunity is bringing you to LA? Working on a cool project or collaboration? I would love to get caught up. Give me a call when you're in town.

From: Fly12271@easymailusa.com – October 16, 2011 – 2:09 PM
To: Renee Greene
Subject: Re: Long time, no talk

Actually, not to freak you out or anything, but what's bringing me to LA is you. Since I have the chance to be in the same place for a while before we start work on a new album in Austin, I thought we might take our "just friends" and see if we could make it "friendlier."

From: Renee Greene – October 16, 2011 – 2:15 PM
To: Fly12271@easymailusa.com
Subject: Re: Long time, no talk

Wow! That's so sweet. I don't really know what to say. Well, I do know what to say. I should tell you that I have been seeing someone for the past couple of months and things are going really well. You would really like him. He's a great guy. Maybe we could all meet up for dinner.

From: Fly12271@easymailusa.com – October 16, 2011 – 2:22 PM
To: Renee Greene
Subject: Re: Long time, no talk

Of course you met someone and of course things are going well. I guess it was just wishful thinking on my part. And as much as I would like to see you, I don't really want to meet the "great guy" you're seeing.

From: Renee Greene – October 16, 2011 – 2:25 PM
To: Fly12271@easymailusa.com
Subject: Re: Long time, no talk

Of course. I'm sorry. I'm just not very good at this stuff.

From: Fly12271@easymailusa.com – October 16, 2011 – 2:28 PM
To: Renee Greene
Subject: Re: Long time, no talk

No worries. I hope he makes you happy. You deserve it.

From: Renee Greene – October 16, 2011 – 2:30 PM
To: Fly12271@easymailusa.com
Subject: Re: Long time, no talk

Thanks Jason. Good luck to you too.

From: Renee Greene – October 16, 2011 – 2:32 PM
To: Shelley Manning
Subject: Disbelief…Total Disbelief!

WHY AREN'T YOU ANSWERING YOUR PHONE?!?!?

OMG! You will NEVER believe who just emailed me. Never, never, ever!

From: Shelley Manning – October 17, 2011 – 8:56 AM
To: Renee Greene
Subject: Re: Disbelief…Total Disbelief!

Sorry. Rest of the weekend got CRAZY. Friday was a major company meeting, followed by a company dinner, followed by a company guy that lasted until the wee hours of this morning. From now on, he will be known as Marathon Man. Anyway, I'm curious to know who emailed you. Queen Elizabeth? Elton John? Justin Beiber? Who, damit, who?

From: Renee Greene – October 17, 2011 – 9:17 AM
To: Shelley Manning
Subject: Re: Disbelief…Total Disbelief!

Jason!

From: Shelley Manning – October 17, 2011 – 9:18 AM
To: Renee Greene
Subject: Re: Disbelief…Total Disbelief!

Jason….???

From: Renee Greene – October 17, 2011 – 9:19 AM
To: Shelley Manning
Subject: Re: Disbelief…Total Disbelief!

Kite! Jason Kite just emailed me.

From: Shelley Manning – October 17, 2011 – 9:19 AM
To: Renee Greene
Subject: Re: Disbelief…Total Disbelief!

Whoa!

From: Renee Greene – October 17, 2011 – 9:22 AM
To: Shelley Manning
Subject: Re: Disbelief…Total Disbelief!

Yeah, and get this. He is thinking of coming to LA for a "while" because of me.

From: Shelley Manning – October 17, 2011 – 9:24 AM
To: Renee Greene
Subject: Re: Disbelief…Total Disbelief!

Really?!? Things are getting VERY interesting! What did you say?

From: Renee Greene – October 17, 2011 – 9:31 AM
To: Shelley Manning
Subject: Re: Disbelief…Total Disbelief!

Well, what could I say? I mean things with Ethan are still in the "new" stage, but they are going great. I don't want to do anything to mess that up. But I must say it sure was flattering to have a talented, famous and totally hot rock star want to move to LA for little ol' me. So, I told him that I was seeing someone and he wished me luck and happiness.

From: Shelley Manning – October 17, 2011 – 9:35 AM
To: Renee Greene
Subject: Re: Disbelief…Total Disbelief!

Well, good for you. Not many ladies get to say they turned down a rock star. Not that you're that petty. But I am. ;)

From: Renee Greene – October 17, 2011 – 9:58 AM
To: PBCupLover@easymailusa.com
Subject: Little Bribery/Lotta Groveling

About to hop on a marathon conference call with the client from hell but wanted to let you know what I have in my hot little hands. Two tickets to the hottest show in town starring the original Broadway cast including one Kristin Chenowith. Now granted, it's a Sunday matinee. But they are orchestra center. That's how I roll! Don't ask me how I got them. Involved a little bribery and a lot of groveling. But nothing illegal. Will pick you up at 1:00. The show starts at 2:00. Hurrah!

From: PBCupLover@easymailusa.com – October 17, 2011 – 10:41 AM
To: Renee Greene
Subject: Re: Little Bribery/Lotta Groveling

Crap! I just tried you, but you're on a call. This Sunday is the Buckeyes game and some of the guys are coming over. I didn't realize you were getting tickets for *this* weekend. Are you totally pissed? Do you want me to cancel my plans?

From: Renee Greene – October 17, 2011 – 10:45 AM
To: PBCupLover@easymailusa.com
Subject: Re: Little Bribery/Lotta Groveling

I'm not pissed. Just bummed out. No, don't cancel on your buddies. I'll take my best friend.

From: PBCupLover@easymailusa.com – October 17, 2011 – 10:48 AM
To: Renee Greene
Subject: Re: Little Bribery/Lotta Groveling

You are amazing! Talk with you later.

From: Renee Greene – October 17, 2011 – 10:53 AM
To: Shelley Manning
Subject: Fwd: Re: Little Bribery/Lotta Groveling

Guess you're in. Pick you up at 1:00?

From: Shelley Manning – October 17, 2011 – 11:51 AM
To: Renee Greene
Subject: Re: Fwd: Re: Little Bribery/Lotta Groveling

Excellent. And how do you really feel?

From: Renee Greene – October 17, 2011 – 11:58 AM
To: Shelley Manning
Subject: Re: Fwd: Re: Little Bribery/Lotta Groveling

Totally bummed. Of course I'm glad you and I will get to see the show. But, honestly plagued by self doubt. Is this a sign he doesn't want to see me anymore? Is this a Matt-style blow off all over again? Should I be offended he would rather hang out with his friends than with me? And why hasn't he introduced me to his friends yet?

From: Shelley Manning – October 17, 2011 – 12:07 PM
To: Renee Greene
Subject: Re: Fwd: Re: Little Bribery/Lotta Groveling

Well, why haven't you introduced him to us yet? What's good for the goose, sweetie. And don't be so paranoid. It's a guy thing. Sundays in the fall = football and beer. Don't read too much into it.

From: Renee Greene – October 17, 2011 – 12:15 PM
To: Shelley Manning
Subject: Re: Fwd: Re: Little Bribery/Lotta Groveling

You're right. I'm letting my mind get the best of me. And a week from Saturday night we are all going out for dinner for Mark's birthday. So you will meet him then. Hurrah!

From: Renee Greene – October 19, 2010 – 4:42 PM
To: Greg_Gordon@excelpaint19875x.com
Subject: Great to see you!

Greg Gordon! I can't believe it. What an amazing coincidence running into you at Excel Paint today. In the four years that I've worked on the account and been there countless time for meetings, I can't believe we haven't bumped into each other before. So you're a scientist. Fantastic! As you saw, I'm a public relations director who works on Excel among other accounts. After college, I ended up moving cross country to work for a major PR firm in New York and then returned to LA to be near my family about four years ago. I'm dating a wonderful guy and having a great time hanging with friends and enjoying all of the fun Los Angeles has to offer. Hope you are finding much happiness and success.

From: Renee Greene – October 19, 2010 – 4:44 PM
To: Ashley Price
Subject: Blast from the past

So, I'm at a meeting at Excel Paint this morning and I bumped into…drum roll, please…Greg Gordon! Can you believe it?

From: Ashley Price – October 19, 2010 – 4:45 PM
To: Renee Greene
Subject: Re: Blast from the past

Who?

From: Renee Greene – October 19, 2010 – 4:47 PM
To: Ashley Price
Subject: Re: Blast from the past

Greg Gordon. We went to junior high and high school with him. He was a science wiz, which is fitting because now he's a scientist for Excel Paint.

From: Ashley Price – October 19, 2010 – 6:56 PM
To: Renee Greene
Subject: Re: Blast from the past

I can't put a finger on it. Let me check the yearbook. Oh yeah, I kind of remember him. So he's a scientist. I didn't realize you needed scientists to make paint.

From: Renee Greene – October 20, 2010 – 9:02 AM
To: Ashley Price
Subject: Re: Blast from the past

Oh yeah, it's very scientific and has to do with nanotechnology. I don't understand it all, but apparently it's big business.

From: Greg_Gordon@excelpaint19875x.com – October 20, 2010 – 9:16 AM
To: Renee Greene
Subject: Re: Great to see you!

Great seeing you yesterday, Renee. You haven't changed a bit since junior high. Can you believe that's how long we've known each other?!

Yes, I'm a molecular chemist at Excel and have been here since graduating from college.

Speaking of which, I should inform you that my mom no longer sends me shoes in the mail. I still remember that day when you laughed uncontrollably when I opened the shoe box in the dorms! Nice to catch up with you ,and take care.

From: Renee Greene – October 20, 2010 – 10:03 AM
To: Greg_Gordon@excelpaint19875x.com
Subject: Re: Great to see you!

I have no recollection of this alleged "shoes by mail" mocking incident. Isn't it funny what we remember…and forget? But, since you so vividly recall it, it must be true. So, I must offer my sincerest apologies to you. I can't even IMAGINE why that would have been wildly funny.

From: Greg_Gordon@excelpaint19875x.com – October 20, 2010 – 10:32 AM
To: Renee Greene
Subject: Re: Great to see you!

I do remember it vividly because you could not stop laughing. And then you told me that – unbeknownst to me – running around junior high and high school was one of your friends – Ashley – who completely despised me for being a "mama's boy" and would mock me behind my back. I found it so surprising that someone I remember seeing for years but never really exchanged words with could hate me so much. Not that I'm harboring any ill will. I just remember the day because it was so shocking.

From: Renee Greene – October 20, 2010 – 10:57 AM
To: Greg_Gordon@excelpaint19875x.com
Subject: Re: Great to see you!

I'm horrified to read your email. I can't believe I was so mean. Some good-natured ribbing about shoes by mail is one thing. Heck! You were ahead of the curve: I love getting shoes in the mail. These days, Zappos rocks! But I can't believe I told you that Ashley hated you. I'm sincerely sorry, not only that she was cruel but that I told you about it. I had a pretty miserable childhood school experience (not that I'm using that as an excuse.) But in my adult years, I've prided myself on having been - for the most part - nice to other people. Now I find out I was just as bad. How awful. Well, perhaps next time I'm at Excel, I can buy you a cup of coffee – but only with a Zappos gift card in tow.

From: Greg_Gordon@excelpaint19875x.com – October 20, 2010 – 11:26 AM
To: Renee Greene
Subject: Re: Great to see you!

Seriously, don't worry about it. You know that crap about what doesn't kill us makes us stronger? Well, let's just say, it works. But I would be happy to grab a coffee with you next time you're at Excel. No gift card needed. Be well.

From: Renee Greene – October 20, 2010 – 11:38 AM
To: Ashley Price
Subject: We suck!!!

So I've been emailing a bit with Greg and apparently we were awful – just awful – to him growing up. You hated him for being a mama's boy and made fun of him behind his back and I told him all about it while we were in college.

Ugh! I feel sick to my stomach. After surviving "Mean April" in grade school, I really prided myself on being a nice person because I understood how cruel kids could be. Now I find out I was just as much of a bitch.

From: Ashley Price – October 20, 2010 – 12:12 PM
To: Renee Greene
Subject: Re: We suck!!!

You aren't a bitch! Kids can sometimes be cruel and we were kids. But honestly, I doubt you were anything but the lovely, wonderfully nice person you are today. Knowing you as I do, this will probably eat away at you for days. You can beat yourself up over lunch at Mel's. See you tomorrow at noon.

From: Renee Greene – October 21, 2010 – 2:45 PM
To: Ashley Price
Subject: Re: We suck!!!

Thanks for our talk at lunch. I do feel a bit better about things. It was a long time ago and I wasn't the mature adult I am today. Okay, so I'm not all that "mature," but at least I am a good person and do my best to treat others nicely. Thanks for letting me work through it all. I feel like I should be paying you for a therapy session.

From: Ashley Price – October 22, 2010 – 10:05 AM
To: Renee Greene
Subject: Re: We suck!!!

Consider ourselves even. Plenty of times, a heart-to-heart with you has helped me as well. Believe me.

From: PBCupLover@easymailusa.com – October 23, 2011 – 2:38 PM
To: Renee Greene
Subject: You are Amazing!!!!!

You are still at the show, but I needed to tell you right away: YOU ARE AMAZING! When the buzzer rang and the guys heard it was you, they started grumbling about the "clingy girl who couldn't let me have ONE day with my friends." But after I returned from downstairs with your homemade cookies (which, by the way, were even better than advertised) and explained that you wouldn't *even* come up to say a quick hello because you didn't want to interrupt our fun, I was dubbed the luckiest SOB on the planet and you were crowned the coolest chick ever.

From: Renee Greene – October 23, 2011 – 4:07 PM
To: PBCupLover@easymailusa.com
Subject: Re: You are Amazing!!!!!

<blush>

From: Renee Greene – October 25, 2011 – 8:26 AM
To: Shelley Manning, Ashley Price, Mark Finlay
Subject: Spoooooky!

Just wanted to see if anyone has anything fun planned for Halloween. It's on a Monday this year, which kind of puts a damper on festivities. I'm thinking of just staying in and handing out candy in my building with Ethan. Anyone want to convince me otherwise – or join us?

From: Mark Finlay – October 25, 2011 – 11:26 AM
To: Renee Greene; Shelley Manning, Ashley Price,
Subject: Re: Spoooooky!

Slammed with work. Major deadline on the game. Saving up all of my free time for my birthday. Sorry Renee.

From: Ashley Price – October 25, 2011 – 12:32 PM
To: Renee Greene; Shelley Manning, Mark Finlay
Subject: Re: Spoooooky!

Ditto for me. Too busy with work and such. But happy to celebrate Mark's birthday in a few weeks.

From: Shelley Manning – October 25, 2011 – 1:27 PM
To: Renee Greene, Ashley Price, Mark Finlay
Subject: Re: Spoooooky!

I have a date with a handsome doctor I met through Tiffany of all people. I'm going to a costume party at the hospital. He's planning to wear army fatigue bottoms and a regular shirt. I'm planning to wear an army fatigue shirt with regular bottoms. And together, we will be an upper and lower GI. I think the hospital folk will get a big kick out of that. And, hopefully later, I'll be wearing nothing at all. ;)!!!!!

From: Shelley Manning – October 25, 2011 – 1:28 PM
To: Renee Greene
Subject: Fwd: Re: Spoooooky!

Oops. Didn't mean to hit "reply to all" on that one. Oh well.

From: Ashley Price – October 25, 2011 – 2:22 PM
To: Renee Greene
Subject: Re: Spoooooky!

Hate to sound judgmental, but not surprising at all. Maybe I should go as Shelley for Halloween. I could just jump anything that walks by. ;)

From: Renee Greene – October 25, 2011 – 2:25 PM
To: Ashley Price
Subject: Re: Spoooooky!

Between you and me, we could all use a little Shelley in us.

From: Ashley Price – October 25, 2011 – 2:28 PM
To: Renee Greene
Subject: Re: Spoooooky!

Well, Mark's had a little Shelley in him and how'd that work out for him? Oh! Did I really just say that?

From: Renee Greene– October 25, 2011 – 2:31 PM
To: Ashley Price
Subject: Re: Spoooooky!

Yes you did, you saucy little minx, you.

From: Renee Greene – November 2, 2011 – 9:15 AM
To: Shelley Manning, Ashley Price
Subject: Lunch Reminder

Just a reminder that we are meeting at Mel's today. See you ladies later.

From: Renee Greene – November 5, 2011 – 9:57 AM
To: Shelley Manning
Subject: FUCK!

Fuck! Fuck, fuck, fuck! I gave Ethan the key to my apartment and you would have thought I gave him a million dollars. He was so cute and sweet and said he was so happy things were going so well. We had a wonderful night and were planning to head over to John O'Lakes for breakfast. I hopped into the shower and when I got out, the key was on the counter, he was nowhere to be found and there was a blinking light on my answering machine.

The message said, "Hi Rene. It's me, Jason. I'm in LA now and wanted to give you a call after we emailed. I know there's this other guy involved, but I was hoping we could still meet for a drink or dinner or something and talk about us. So, give me a call. You have the number."

Fuck! I've tried him like 10 times and he won't pick up the phone. What do I do? What do I do?

Why aren't you home?!?!?!

From: Shelley Manning – November 5, 2011 – 11:02 AM
To: Renee Greene
Subject: Re: FUCK!

Oy! Sorry. Have been hanging out with a friend. A female friend. Yes, believe it or not, I have female friends AND other friends besides you. I'm leaving in 30 and will call you from the car.

From: Renee Greene – November 5, 2011 – 11:05 AM
To: PBCupLover@easymailusa.com
Subject: Please Call Me!!!

We need to talk. Please call me.

From: Renee Greene – November 5, 2011 – 5:30 PM
To: PBCupLover@easymailusa.com
Subject: Please Read Me!!!

Okay if you won't talk to me, at least read this and give me a chance to explain. Before we met, I went on ONE date with this guy named Jason. He kind of has this crazy lifestyle where he travels a lot and we decided that it would be better to just stay friends than to try a long distance thing. He emailed a few days ago that he was going to be in LA for a while and wanted to try and pick back up where we had originally started. I told him that I had met a WONDERFUL guy and was TOTALLY HAPPY so thanks anyway. I haven't spoken to him since. I would never cheat on you. Please call me. I would hate for this to end over some silly misunderstanding.

From: PBCupLover@easymailusa.com – November 5, 2011 – 5:42 PM
To: Renee Greene
Subject: Re: Please Read Me!!!

After everything I told you about Katarina, I can't believe you wouldn't tell me that some old boyfriend wanted to get back together with you. This will never work if I can't trust you.

From: Renee Greene – November 5, 2011 – 5:45 PM
To: PBCupLover@easymailusa.com
Subject: Re: Please Read Me!!!

He wasn't an ex-boyfriend. We went on ONE date. And, we didn't even sleep together. I just didn't think it was important.

From: PBCupLover@easymailusa.com – November 5, 2011 – 5:46 PM
To: Renee Greene
Subject: Re: Please Read Me!!!

Not important? Maybe we have different ideas about what's important in a relationship.

From: Renee Greene – November 5, 2011 – 5:48 PM
To: PBCupLover@easymailusa.com
Subject: Re: Please Read Me!!!

Okay. You're right. I should have told you. I just didn't want you to get weirded out.

From: PBCupLover@easymailusa.com – November 5, 2011 – 5:50 PM
To: Renee Greene
Subject: Re: Please Read Me!!!

Weirded out? Why do I feel like there's something you aren't telling me?

From: Renee Greene – November 5, 2011 – 5:54 PM
To: PBCupLover@easymailusa.com
Subject: Re: Please Read Me!!!

Well, I met him backstage in the VIP area of a client event. Everyone was being really snobby to the lowly PR person working there, but he was really nice, chatting away and then asked for my card. He called me. We had one date. He was going away for a while for work and that was it.

From: PBCupLover@easymailusa.com – November 5, 2011 – 5:55 PM
To: Renee Greene
Subject: Re: Please Read Me!!!

So, that's the WHOLE story?

From: Renee Greene – November 5, 2011 – 5:57 PM
To: PBCupLover@easymailusa.com
Subject: Re: Please Read Me!!!

His name is Jason Kite and he's the bassist for Marsh 7.

From: PBCupLover@easymailusa.com – November 5, 2011 – 5:59 PM
To: Renee Greene
Subject: Re: Please Read Me!!!

The Jason Kite? Jason Kite wants to start up a relationship with you?

From: Renee Greene – November 5, 2011 – 6:02 PM
To: PBCupLover@easymailusa.com
Subject: Re: Please Read Me!!!

What? You don't think a cool rock star would like an average girl like me?

From: PBCupLover@easymailusa.com – November 5, 2011 – 6:07 PM
To: Renee Greene
Subject: Re: Please Read Me!!!

Renee, you're *anything* but average! (You're a supermodel, after all!) It doesn't surprise me at all. I guess I'm just a bit blown away that with a choice between me and a famous musician, you would want to be with a lowly financial analyst.

From: Renee Greene – November 5, 2011 – 6:09 PM
To: PBCupLover@easymailusa.com
Subject: Re: Please Read Me!!!

Well, I do choose you! If you will still have me. Otherwise, I've got a call to return. ;)

From: PBCupLover@easymailusa.com – November 5, 2011 – 6:11 PM
To: Renee Greene
Subject: Re: Please Read Me!!!

The only call you make better be to me. In fact, I'm dialing you now…

From: Renee Greene – November 6, 2011 – 8:25 AM
To: Shelley Manning
Subject: All is well!

Crisis averted! Whew! I'm telling you, for a minute there, I thought it was over. O-V-E-R. Over! But we talked and things are cool now.

From: Shelley Manning – November 7, 2011 – 7:58 AM
To: Renee Greene
Subject: Re: All is well!

Did you at least have some awesome make-up sex?

From: Renee Greene – November 7, 2011 – 8:26 AM
To: Shelley Manning
Subject: Re: All is well!

Only you, Shelley, would ask that. Only you. And the answer is yes. :)

CHAPTER NINE – IT'S A SMALL WORLD AFTER ALL

From: Mark Finlay – November 8, 2011 – 8:26 AM
To: Renee Greene, Shelley Manning, Ashley Price
Subject: Celebrate Good Times, C'mon!

Okay, so the plan is to meet a Henri's at 9:00 sharp for my birthday. I've reserved the private room, so it should be perfect. I'm really glad the three of you will be there. Below is the link to the evite that I sent to everyone else.

From: Renee Greene – November 8, 2011 – 9:42 AM
To: Mark Finlay, Shelley Manning, Ashley Price
Subject: Re: Celebrate Good Times, C'mon!

Can't wait to celebrate with you Saturday night, Mark!!! And you are finally going to meet Ethan. YEAH! I think you guys are going to really like him. At least I hope so. I've told him how important it is for me that all of you approve. He's wonderful. He's smart, witty and a ton of fun. I'm telling you, I could just lie in bed, in his arms, all morning. (Sorry if that's a bit TMI for you, Mark.) I know this is going to sound crazy, but I've fallen in love with him. I can't believe I'm saying that out loud – well, typing it out loud–well, you know what I mean. Can't wait. See you guys at Henri's at 9:00.

From: Shelley Manning – November 8, 2011 – 10:07 AM
To: Renee Greene
Subject: Bribes

Getting in good with me will be critical for his future success with you. Please advise him that some of my favorite bribes include chocolate truffles, diamonds and, of course, good ol' hard currency. If he's really up for the challenge, he'll have to cough up the goods.

From: Renee Greene – November 8, 2011 – 10:42 AM
To: Shelley Manning
Subject: Re: Bribes

Whew....you are a tough cookie! Though before he starts bribing you with diamonds, he better throw some of them my way first!!!!!! Not that I'm the original "material girl" or anything (really, no need to call me Madonna) but geez, I ain't above it either. Tee Hee!

From: Renee Greene – November 10, 2011 – 2:14 PM
To: Ashley Price
Subject: Say what?!?

You and Greg Gordon!?! How and when did that happen? Details, please.

From: Ashley Price – November 10, 2011 – 3:18 PM
To: Renee Greene
Subject: Re: Say what?!?

I really took our discussion about me unfairly judging you with the online dating to heart. (Good to know I'm actually listening, right?)

Well, anyway, after you emailed and explained how terrible I was to him in school, I felt really badly. So I called Excel, got his email address and sent an apology. The apology turned into coffee, which turned into dinner, which turned into breakfast. (DON'T, I REPEAT, DON'T TELL SHELLEY!) From there, we just started seeing each other regularly and things are going really well. I didn't want to say anything this early and risk jinxing things. How did you find out?

From: Renee Greene – November 10, 2011 – 4:07 PM
To: Ashley Price
Subject: Re: Say what?!?

I saw the two of you conoodling together over pasta primavera at Max Stanton's. I was in such a state of shock, I didn't come over to say hello. But, I must say I'm very happy for you. Love certainly works in strange ways, don't you think?

From: Ashley Price – November 10, 2011 – 4:08 PM
To: Renee Greene
Subject: Re: Say what?!?

Indeed! <u>We</u> will see you at Mark's party on Saturday.

From: Mark Finlay – November 12, 2011 – 8:26 AM
To: Renee Greene, Shelley Manning, Ashley Price
Subject: Re: Celebrate Good Times, C'mon!

See you peeps tonight. Okay, clearly I cannot get away with saying "peeps." Sounds ridiculous. Let me try it again. See you lovely ladies tonight.

From: PBCupLover@easymailusa.com – November 12, 2011 – 10:02 PM
To: Renee Greene
Subject: Trying to reach you

I've been trying to call you. I'm certain you're home. Please pick up the phone or call me back. I need to talk with you.

From: Ashley Price – November 12, 2011 – 11:14 PM
To: Renee Greene
Subject: I'm worried

Renee. I've been calling and calling. But you haven't returned my call. I'm getting worried. Will you call me!

From: Shelley Manning – November 12, 2011 – 11:45 PM
To: Renee Greene
Subject: Let's Talk

Renee. I've left you like a gazillion messages. Pick up the phone. We need to talk.

From: PBCupLover@easymailusa.com – November 13, 2011 – 12:20 AM
To: Renee Greene
Subject: COPS!

Okay. I've just come home after 20 minutes of pounding on your front door. I would have pounded longer but your neighbors looked like they were going to call the cops. Let's just say if they did, YOU would be my one phone call from jail. Please, call me!

From: Shelley Manning – November 13, 2011 – 4:00 AM
To: Renee Greene
Subject: CALL ME!!!

Renee. You are being ridiculous. CALL ME!

From: Shelley Manning – November 13, 2011 – 7:43 AM
To: Renee Greene
Subject: C'Mon!

Pick up the goddam phone, Renee!!!

From: Mark Finlay – November 13, 2011 – 9:02 AM
To: Renee Greene
Subject: You okay?

Hi. Are you okay? You seemed kind of upset last night and then I didn't see you before you left. Wanted to make sure you got home okay.

From: Renee Greene – November 13, 2011 – 10:45 AM
To: Mark Finlay
Subject: Re: You okay?

Hi Mark. Sorry I had to run out of your birthday celebration. I hope you had a great evening.

From: Shelley Manning – November 13, 2011 – 10:47 AM
To: Renee Greene
Subject: RIDICULOUS! CALL ME!

Renee Michele Greene! We have been friends too long for you to stay angry at me. And you like Ethan too much to let this come between you. It's not that big of a deal. I've left like a gazillion messages for you. We need to talk. CALL ME!!!!!

From: Mark Finlay – November 13, 2011 – 10:48 AM
To: Renee Greene
Subject: Re: You okay?

It was great fun. But, what happened to you? You were upset. Is everything okay?

From: Renee Greene – November 13, 2011 – 10:51 AM
To: Mark Finlay
Subject: Re: You okay?

Oh, I've probably just lost my best friend and the greatest man I've ever met. But other than that, everything is just peachy.

From: Mark Finlay – November 13, 2011 – 10:55 AM
To: Renee Greene
Subject: Re: You okay?

What happened? You and Ethan seemed so happy. Did he hurt you? Do I need to go and kick his ass? (I knew you needed a good laugh!)

From: Renee Greene – November 13, 2011 – 11:06 AM
To: Mark Finlay
Subject: Re: You okay?

Tee Hee! That was actually hilarious. I haven't smiled in more than a day. So thank you. No, Ethan didn't do anything. He's wonderful and I'm just a horrible, horrible person. You know what, I really just don't feel like talking about this right now. Listen, I will call you later. I just need some time alone, okay?

From: Mark Finlay– November 13, 2011 – 11:15 AM
To: Renee Greene
Subject: Re: You okay?

Of course. But I could easily see how happy Ethan has made you. And, not to get all mushy on you, but that's the kind of relationship I really want to find. I figure if I put half as much energy into finding a girlfriend as I do writing code, I should be able to find the right one. So, that's my goal for my 30th year. A birthday present from you to me and from me to me.

From: Renee Greene – November 13, 2011 – 11:17 AM
To: Mark Finlay
Subject: Re: You okay?

You're great, Mark. I know if you try, you'll find what you're looking for. I'll call you later.

From: Renee Greene – November 13, 2011 – 11:19 AM
To: Ashley Price
Subject: Re: I'm worried

Sorry. I didn't mean for you to worry. I just really don't want to talk on the phone. I can't believe this. I just can't believe this. Of all the men out there, why does Ethan have to be the Cuddler? Why? Why can't I for once, just once, be happy?

From: Ashley Price – November 13, 2011 – 11:25 AM
To: Renee Greene
Subject: Re: I'm worried

Why does it surprise you that Ethan and Shelley slept together? She's slept with half of Los Angeles! She hooked up with *Mark*! You just said you were in love with this man. You can't let this ruin a great relationship. It's not easy to meet someone in this lifetime, and I should know. You've been blessed to meet someone you really could have a future with. Just call him and sort it out.

From: Renee Greene – November 13, 2011 – 11:42 AM
To: Ashley Price
Subject: Re: I'm worried

But, he's the Cuddler. We made fun of him! I made fun of him. How do I look at him, hold him, kiss him, be with him when I know how horrible I've been? I thought I felt bad about Greg Gordon. This is 100 times worse!
I'm a bad, bad person. And how do I see him and Shelley without picturing them together? I'm just…oh I don't know. I'm just so guilty, confused, hurt, angry, depressed. I just need time to sort this thing out.

From: Ashley Price – November 13, 2011 – 12:25 PM
To: Renee Greene
Subject: Re: I'm worried

Far be it for me to judge, but if you want my advice, I say GET OVER YOURSELF. You are not a bad person. Okay, so you were being a little petty – haven't we all at some point or another? But you have met a wonderful man who is crazy about you. You need to call him, tell him you are sorry and move on. As for Shelley, I can't believe this has never happened to you before. Never once, not even in college, did she make a move on someone you liked or did you two go out with someone in common? She's never been my favorite person in the world, as I'm sure you've guessed by now. But, I must admit, she has been a good friend to you as long as I've known her. I think you need to get past this.

From: Renee Greene – November 13, 2011 – 12:38 PM
To: Ashley Price
Subject: Re: I'm worried

No. We did have a big fight sophomore year. I really liked this guy named Brad who lived upstairs from us. He had curly blond hair and woke up every morning at 5:30 to go surfing. He would come home just as I was getting up to have breakfast before my 8:00 class. He'd walk by all moist and sandy. We flirted a lot, but nothing had ever happened.

Well, that Halloween we decided to throw a rockin' costume party. I came as a devil and she dressed as an angel. (Ha! Talk about role reversal.) Anyway, I went into the store room to get some more toilet paper and saw them making out. I was FURIOUS.

She claimed to be really drunk and didn't realize that he was the guy in the George Bush mask. But, I kind of suspected that she did really know and just wanted to prove that she could get anyone, even someone that I liked. But she apologized and said it would never happen again. I forgave her, and up until now, there's never been another issue.

From: Ashley Price – November 13, 2011 – 12:47 PM
To: Renee Greene
Subject: Re: I'm worried

Well, you forgave her once. And this time, she didn't even know you were going to meet Ethan six months later. So, why can't you forgive her now?

From: Renee Greene – November 13, 2011 – 12:55 PM
To: Ashley Price
Subject: Re: I'm worried

I suppose because with Brad, it was no big deal. Yeah, I liked him and we flirted. But really, it was not going anywhere serious. But with Ethan, I see myself with him. Getting married. Having babies. Growing old. I see it all. And the thought that I'll have to look at him and picture the two of them together for the rest of my life may just be too much to bear. And, knowing how horrible I've been to him, even though he didn't know it…well, I just can't stand it and what it says about me.

From: Ashley Price – November 13, 2011 – 1:04 PM
To: Renee Greene
Subject: Re: I'm worried

Renee. Listen to me. I may not be an expert on romance and love. Lord knows I haven't had a successful relationship since...well, never. Although I'm really trying with Greg! But I'm telling you. You and Ethan are meant to be together. You and Shelley are great friends. You have to get past this. I know it hurts and I know it is going to be hard. But love is worth it. Love for this great man. And love for your good friend.

From: Renee Greene – November 13, 2011 – 1:10 PM
To: Ashley Price
Subject: Re: I'm worried

You're right. Thank you for being such a good friend yourself. For listening to me whine and complain and for offering such good advice. Okay. I'm going to have one last really good cry and then call Ethan. I'll let you know how it goes.

From: PBCupLover@easymailusa.com – November 13, 2011 – 1:30 PM
To: Renee Greene
Subject: My POV!

This is getting crazy. We need to talk about this. Okay. So you won't listen to what I have to say. Well, then at least read it. I don't understand why this is such a big deal to you.

Shelley and I went out like half a dozen times...months ago. I don't want to say it didn't mean *anything* because I know Shelley is your friend and that would be insulting to her and you. But I don't want for you to think it meant *everything,* because it didn't. We had fun and she is a great gal. I can understand why you guys are such good friends. And, yes, this is a bit awkward.

But if you're worried about how I feel about you in comparison to my feelings for her, there is NOTHING to be worried about. I didn't feel for her anywhere near what I'm feeling for you. Not even close.

Renee, I'm in love with you. Do you hear (or should I say read) that? I'm in LOVE with you. Not the, I'm-having-some-fun-with-a-cool-gal-around-town feeling. This is love. Deep. Real. Raw. Heartfelt.

I think you are the most beautiful, special, hilarious, dazzling, compassionate, insanely wonderful person I've ever met. (And it's not just your great chocolate chip cookies.) It's everything about you. It's the fact that you get lost coming home from the neighborhood grocery store where you shop every week. It's how you laugh at my incredibly lame puns and jokes not because you want to humor me but because you think I'm actually funny. It's that you tell your nephew, "when mommy and daddy say no, Auntie Renee will always say yes." It's everything and you're everything.

Please, please don't let this end just because I happened to go on a few dates with your friend a long time ago. This is too special to lose. I'm home. I'm sitting by the phone. Please call me.

From: Renee Greene – November 14, 2011 – 9:00 AM
To: Ashley Price
Subject: Sorry!

Sorry, I woke you. I didn't realize I was calling you at 3:00 a.m. Ethan finally fell asleep and I wanted to let you know how things went. Of course, I didn't realize what time it was. Sorry. I'm home now and I figured you might be sleeping in, since you were so rudely awakened so very early. Anyway, I'm exhausted. Mentally and physically exhausted. We talked for hours. Now normally, we talk for hours. Which is one of the reasons I love him so much. We can literally talk for hours about, well, just about anything. But this was brutal. I mean we talked and cried and talked some more FOR HOURS.

It started out with him totally apologizing to ME for having had a "relationship" – yes he used the pantomime quotation marks – with Shelley. Can you believe it? He was apologizing TO ME(!) for not having the foresight to realize that months later he would meet me.

Of course that made me feel even guiltier. I told him that I wasn't upset about him and Shelley and that he had nothing to be sorry for. I then completely broke down into heaving sobs and confessed all about the Cuddler. He sat there silent while I detailed every joke made at his expense and begged and groveled for him not to hate me. Then he just looked at me blankly.

I thought for sure he was going to tell me I was a wicked person and that he never wanted to see me again. Then he looked at me with this incredulous expression on his face and said, "That's what this is all about?" I tearfully said yes and he said, "Okay. You're forgiven. Now, let's order Chinese."

Then he just held me for what seemed like hours but was actually like 20 minutes. But for me to stay silent and let someone just hold me for 20 minutes seemed like an eternity. And it was awesome. I was feeling so guilty for the things I said before I even knew who he was and with his calm and gentle forgiveness, he made me, for just a moment, feel like ten times more guilty. But then I realized that he just really loves me and that it was quite obviously nothing personal because I really love him too. So now I'm home and need to call Shelley. I think this one might be even more exhausting. But I wanted to let you know that everything with Ethan is fine. I'll let you know how things with Shelley go.

From: Shelley Manning – November 15, 2011 – 1:30 PM
To: Ashley Price
Subject: Thank you!!!!!

Ashley: I just wanted to say thank you for encouraging Renee to finally call me back and work through this whole thing. I know we haven't always seen eye-to-eye on things. But, I really appreciate your recognizing how much I love her and that I would never intentionally hurt her. She called last night and we worked through everything. So, thanks.

From: Ashley Price – November 15, 2011 – 1:52 PM
To: Shelley Manning
Subject: Re: Thank you!!!!!

It was my pleasure. You're right. We are very different and don't necessarily look at the world through the same perspective.

But despite our differences, we do have a lot in common, most notably our love for that crazy gal. Glad it worked out.

From: Renee Greene – November 16, 2011 – 9:02 AM
To: Ashley Price; Shelley Manning
Subject: Lunch at Mel's

Hi ladies. Hoping we could all meet up for lunch at Mel's tomorrow. Are you in?

From: Ashley Price – November 16, 2011 – 9:07 AM
To: Renee Greene; Shelley Manning
Subject: Re: Lunch at Mel's

Sounds good to me. I always do look forward to lunch with the two of you.

From: Shelley Manning – November 16, 2011 – 9:15 AM
To: Ashley Price; Renee Greene
Subject: Re: Lunch at Mel's

Of course, sweetie. I walked by the other day and saw they had a really great new looking waiter. ;) Mwah! Mwah!

Made in the USA
San Bernardino, CA
31 October 2015